SNAKE CITY

SNAKE CITY

CITY

JOE ROSENBLATT

EXILE
editions

Fiction, Poetry, Translation, Drama and Nonfiction

Library and Archives Canada Cataloguing in Publication

Rosenblatt, Joe, 1933-, author
Snake city / Joe Rosenblatt.

Issued in print and electronic formats.
ISBN 978-1-55096-464-6 (pbk.).--ISBN 978-1-55096-467-7 (pdf).--
ISBN 978-1-55096-465-3 (epub).--ISBN 978-1-55096-466-0 (mobi)

I. Title.

PS8535.O763S63 2015   C813'.6   C2014-908416-1
                                              C2014-908417-X

Copyright © Joe Rosenblatt, 2015
Co-editors Catherine Owen & David Berry

Design and Composition by Mishi Uroboros
Cover of body painted woman by Evgeniya Litovchenko
Typeset in Big Caslon font at Moons of Jupiter Studios

Published by Exile Editions Ltd ~ www.ExileEditions.com
144483 Southgate Road 14 – GD, Holstein, Ontario, N0G 2A0
Printed and Bound in Canada in 2015, by Imprimerie Gauvin

We gratefully acknowledge, for their support toward our publishing activities,
the Canada Council for the Arts, the Government of Canada through
the Canada Book Fund (CBF), the Ontario Arts Council,
and the Ontario Media Development Corporation.

Canadian Sales: The Canadian Manda Group, 664 Annette Street,
Toronto ON M6S 2C8 www.mandagroup.com 416 516 0911

North American and international distribution, and U.S. sales:
Independent Publishers Group, 814 North Franklin Street,
Chicago IL 60610 www.ipgbook.com toll free: 1 800 888 4741

For Milton Acorn,
in memoriam

Prologue

I see a snaky tie suspended from a chrome hanger stir in a clothes closet and fill out as though some spirit is flowing evenly into its digestive tract. Soon I find myself staring into its Stygian mouth. An oscillating forked tongue ribboning in my direction is picking up my scent.

Patterned in lateral bars, Death has morphed into a black silk tie with a triangular-shaped head, its feline-like pupils longing for a Windsor knot to accessorize a single-breasted tuxedo jacket with three or four silver monogrammed buttons.

I begin stroking the tie, and to my delight, it starts to purr before falling contentedly asleep.

A Troupe of Visiting Angels

Do angels serving as messengers for the Almighty ever encounter vipers along their delivery route on earth? Let's just say, for example, a troupe of angels is circumnavigating the fringes of a cottonmouth-infested bog, and end up knocking on the cabin door of a long-haired rube named Freddie, a snowbird retiree from Canada, wearing a glazed stare and a brass earring on his chipped left ear.

Months before, while domiciling in a trailer camp, a gnomish Florida land speculator had talked him into purchasing forty acres of wetland complete with brush, decaying pine, and for company, swathes of fireflies blazing in the night in competition with the ghostly whorls of flaming methane from a nearby bog.

"I have a message for you," said the leading angel, introducing himself as Gabriel and ruffling his alabaster white wings.

"Hey, Gabe, I bet you come with a message from the Big Fellow?" said Freddie, gesturing a bent digit toward the sky. Blanching at the nickname, Gabriel kept his composure and replied, "None other, brother."

Freddie, in a vague attempt to be a genial host, was about to welcome the fluffy delegation into his dwelling when an unexpected complication crinkled his hosting propriety.

The blackest and seemingly meanest viper came out to meet his guests. The cottonmouth opened his mouth, exposing a puffy white interior, and let out a loud defensive hiss just as Freddie beckoned his callers to come inside the cabin. "Pay him no heed. He's venom-free. Why, only this morning I squeezed his cuspies real hard. Not a toxic drop in this bugger. Don't be scared, why he's just a pussycat." The angels, however, weren't entirely convinced that Freddie's companion was as friendly as he claimed.

"What's his name?" asked Gabriel, trying not to betray his fear.

"Why, Gabe, I just call him plain Cottonmouth. Now just look at his gums, don't they look like cotton?" replied Freddie with a shrug and a smile that didn't sit quite right on his face. "Now," he added, "I thought I'd name him after my dad, but heck, Cottonmouth is just fine."

Things weren't going well for Freddie. Cottonmouth's elliptical cat-like eyes began to glow a deep magenta and soon a few of the angels began whispering that the devil had cleverly morphed into a serpent. Freddie, they suspected, was bedding down with the King of Hell, yet there was no mark of the beast on either Freddie's hands, knuckles, or on his forehead. Cottonmouth became increasingly apprehensive of Gabriel's frightful stare.

He had seen that look of terror before in the eyes of a swamp rat. Zapped by Cottonmouth's hypnotic gaze, that rodent had frozen in his tracks before being pounced upon and ingurgitated greedily, a very satisfying meal. Cottonmouth couldn't understand why Freddie ate dead meat when the taste sensation was in gorging on animated prey squealing for its life.

Freddie's ears began to itch as the angels conveyed their Master's displeasure at Freddie's taking up with a wild bog woman whom the locals called Hilda. Attired in a dress woven together from alligator weed, dog fennel, swamp lilies and red mango leaves, Hilda proved to be a natural couturière. Her outfit was as organic as the weed he was smoking. Freddie assumed, at first, that she was a demon.

She had suddenly appeared out of nowhere, demanding a puff from his smoking pipe, and with a few more shared puffs it didn't take long for the giggling pair to take to each other like rutting bobcats. It was this brutish activity, Gabriel claimed, which had caused a stye to form in one of the Creator's infinite eyes.

The Lake of Fire

"You'll end up in the Lake of Fire if you don't mend your ways," warned Gabriel, to which Freddie responded, "Now this here lake wouldn't be around these parts, would it now?" Cottonmouth didn't much care for Freddie's guests, and it wasn't so much taking an intense dislike to them; sniffing the lot, he could detect no food value, no presence of protein, especially in Gabriel, who eyed him with such condescension it chilled his scaly skin from the top of his head to the tip of his tail.

He would have enjoyed injecting Gabriel with paralyzing toxin, if only Freddie hadn't milked his venom as he was in the habit of doing each morning, letting the juice run into a clear glass jar he normally used to stir his hooch.

Summoning his inner mojo, Cottonmouth somehow managed to hiss out a voluble warning to the angels before they took flight. Gabriel looked back at Cottonmouth. Gabriel's sunny face, the one he normally used to deliver his Boss's nasty messages to earthly transgressors, blanched a shade whiter than his wings – and for a brief moment, his gown folded funereally into a winding sheet.

The other angels watched in terror, until Gabriel somehow managed to signal them into a flying formation, and in seconds they were skyward bound, heading into passing clouds.

A Roll on an Unmade Bed

Lately, Hilda had taken a shine to Freddie's surging companion, suggesting they take a roll on Freddie's unmade bed. She was all for a round of spiralling sex, except that Freddie balked at Cottonmouth serving as an elasticized ligature that would lash him and Hilda firmly together while they got it on with a fury that would have ignited a column of swamp gas. He proposed, instead, that she continue to lie in ambush for him. Danger was his aphrodisiac; being rolled over in the muck by Hilda excited him to no end.

But Cottonmouth didn't take kindly to their conjugal gymnastics, either on Freddie's bed or on some mud flat overlooking a marsh. Their sexual congress made him nauseous, so much so that he had to chuck the remains of an amphibian his stomach acids had recently liquefied.

Being an ace olfactory wonder, what he couldn't smell instantly disquieted him; associating taste and smell with slow food, he had arrived at the conclusion that his stretchable jaws could neither accommodate Freddie's bulk or the *pièce de résistance* that was Hilda; but it didn't stop his oscillating forked tongue from fanning the fragrances that clung to her like swamp bay magnolia, yellow jasmine, marsh lilies – all of which he inhaled, as well as the pleasant waftings of other exotic wetland blooms. Cottonmouth sensed daunting presences nearby.

Napping on Freddie's bed, his head resting on a pillow, he dreamt of fireflies carrying posterior lanterns which flashed urgent mating calls.

His Free-Range Seismic Tongue

Cottonmouth's reptilian sense of propriety incorporated a standard of hygiene peculiar to the viper tribe: a snakish nest was always clean for hatchlings, unlike Freddie's routinely unmade bed with its patina of excretion and dried spermatozoa.

Freddie and Hilda were viewed by Cottonmouth as no better than a kind of a runny foul-smelling *foie gras* he occasionally spat out after taxing the elasticity of his jaws gorging on a duckling. Also, Cottonmouth thought Hilda's breath was like a swamp flower and, as for Freddie, the snake suspected something had died in his mouth, perhaps one of those rats that lurked about the rube's cabin.

The angels were definitely off his dining radar. Cottonmouth couldn't detect anything meatishly edible in the lot. He hadn't run into their kind cruising for toothsome salt-flavoured prey among the waterlogged mangroves.

His free-range seismic tongue had its penchant for warblers and other wetland fowl, but as a top of the line sensory organ, it favoured Hilda.

He would have devoured her by degrees and enjoyed every morsel. Love for him was a total dining experience. He delighted in the song his stomach acids made breaking down his prey's loveable protein. But when it came to Hilda, he preferred, instead, to feast his eyes on her: she was a scrumptious meal by any other name, a repast to be tongued, fondled, cuddled and squeezed.

The Sanctuary of a Clothes Closet

Unbeknownst to Freddie, Cottonmouth was obsessive about snaky hygiene. As a hatchling, he recalled his mother's pride in maintaining a spotlessly clean nest. In contrast, Freddie's bed was so soiled that Cottonmouth became stricken with fear that he might develop a skin infection.

There were other complications as well. It wasn't Hilda's breath, made more pungent by living off edible swamp flora and the deep orange yolk of mallard, a diet that made Cottonmouth's skin creep; it was Freddie's fetid breath. Cottonmouth suspected a dead mouse had somehow lodged inside his mouth, and often the odour became so offensive that Cottonmouth retreated to the clothes closet.

It was his sanctuary and there he would lie down beneath a line of painted silken ties, each tie depicting a viper's triangular head, gaping mouth, pronounced fangs, and for an optical illusion, a *trompe-l'œil* of rubied eyes.

They appeared to incandesce as though fuelled by a miniscule furnace. Those eyeballs glared down at Cottonmouth as he curled into a ball and fell soundly asleep.

The Pressures of Love

Hilda may have preferred that Freddie hadn't cupped Cotton-mouth's venom for in knowing there was a real possibility she could suffer a fatal bite, her body tingled with excitement. Extreme danger provided a catalyst for a more intense orgasm, but it didn't do a damned thing for Cottonmouth except send him into a deep snake pit of melancholia. And yet, something warm and tender was working its way through his entrails even as he lashed out at her, puncturing her neck, which caused her to spiral, swoon, but not before breaking out into a storm of obscene utterances that would have made a burly teamster blush on a dock.

Through these expletives, her breath began to quicken until it found a momentary repose in a barely audible giggle which served initially to debase Cottonmouth. Yet this abject state was balanced by another feature of his biological needs, buoying him in the next instant to a snakish pride.

His tongue caught a whiff of snake on Hilda and he gradually became overcome by those reptilian fragrances, leading to a state of amorousness, especially heightened when his heat sensors told him that Hilda was glued together by an animated protein substance; still, his desire was not to devour but only exaltedly lick her.

Freddie could only watch in envy what he viewed as the snake's penile elasticity and his own now-failing member.

It was often at these hastily organized threesomes that competitive undercurrents in him led frequently to erectile dysfunction, and it was in such critical situations that she reached for an ornate dildo crafted from the hide of a salt water crocodile. It was an art object which she managed to liberate from the dwelling of one of Freddie's Bible-toting neighbours, Yeshua Possumo, or "Yessie," as he was known in the neighbourhood. Yeshua, he claimed, was Christ's given name.

Freddie thought it odd he took no offence at that irreverent nickname. Yeshua preferred it that way. He wouldn't stand for blasphemers among the swampbillies uttering Christ's first name.

Fetch

"Oh, that is so sweet," Hilda murmured. "Squeeze me again, hon," and she wasn't directing her affections at Freddie but at Cottonmouth, who in an exhausted state managed to slide off the bed and slither to a corner of the cabin, where he collapsed into a heap, his tail wrapped securely around his trembling head.

Finding no response in her plea for Cottonmouth to return to their sweat-drenched love bed and reapply his delicious pressures, she then began deriding Freddie for his poor performance, his gyrating hips having slowed down so drastically they barely moved at all. He was a man in his forties, already in dire need of hormone replacement and the sparkle of Viagra, possibly the two together.

If Freddie's tears had filled a city reservoir, they still wouldn't have quenched Hilda's flamy anger as she questioned his manliness while looking longingly at Cottonmouth. So wildly was she addicted to his amorous compressions, thrilled to the odd love bite, but only if he was venom-free and didn't break her skin causing blood vessel damage with its resultant hematoma. There were limits she set to their frolicking.

Cottonmouth had his passions too. He possessed the intelligence quotient of a Cavalier King Charles Spaniel in sniffing out all the possible places in the cabin that Hilda's pleasure extender could be hiding. Freddie even once tried to hide Hilda's dildo in the cabin, only to have Cottonmouth retrieve it. It was on such occasions that a fleeting thought passed between Freddie's porcine-shaped hairy ears: Cottonmouth would make a fancy belt, with enough skin left over for a nifty tie or two, and hadn't Yessie put in a bid to buy that clever reptile?

Freddie was plainly irritated with Cottonmouth's unsnake-like behaviour, such as when he gripped Hilda's *objet d'art* firmly between his intractable jaws and dropped it on Hilda's lap; further, if playing fetch wasn't enough, he would slither away from the bed, gripping the panties she had woven from bits and pieces of soft-stemmed marshland grass. It titillated Hilda when he stared back at her, contemptuously shaking the garment as he drooled and hissed.

A Prisoner of Love

Cottonmouth, though de-venomed, still had his way of showing his displeasure, even vitriol. He did nip Hilda in the buff but somehow his fangs didn't break her skin, although there was a discernible indentation of two passion bites which bruised her flesh a ripe red, pink and black.

Hilda could tell, in her coquettish aloof way, that Cotton-mouth was deeply enamoured with her. His eyes sparkled in her presence. He wanted to bring her gifts to earn more of her affection, so he seized articles of women's clothes fluttering and drying in the wind on a neighbourhood clothesline. Such is the chemistry that defines a prisoner of love.

He would snatch the garments with his open mouth and, upon securing the looted trove, return to gift it to her, drop it on her lap, and then their amorous gazes would meet in a conjoined illumination, a flash of white light; once, he even presented her with a black stiletto shoe which he drooled on, undulating over that shoe until the leather shone.

She fancied Cottonmouth in a neatly thatched grassy dress. Donning this frock would serve to align the feminine in him to the male side. It activated the bubbling spawn of Hilda's sexual imagination to think of Cottonmouth as a cross-dressing penile-empowered reptile! Meanwhile, jealousy ate through Freddie like black rot through a once robust ruddy tomato.

The Love that Dares Not Speak Its Name

Freddie's impulse to bag Cottonmouth for Yessie grew stronger. He would throw the dildo into the same bag. Gabriel's voice crackled in Freddie's noggin, urging him to bag Hilda as well, though, as Freddie was sweet on Hilda, the latter request was ignored. Freddie assumed the voice in his otherwise silent head was due to something he had previously eaten; and upon further reflection, he repressed his petulance toward Cottonmouth, recognizing it as puerile.

Freddie, after all, was not only an adult but higher on the evolutionary scale, although Cottonmouth wouldn't have thought so. Cottonmouth was only acting out his nature. Not having a dog as a pet, Freddie felt that Cottonmouth was fulfilling a need as a substitute object of affection, an honorary mutt.

He would put Cottonmouth on a leash, maybe take him for a vigorous daily crawl, and then keep him fettered and away from *the love that dare not speak its name*, Hilda's dildo.

Pillow Talk

Freddie was awoken in the small hours of the morning by a voice in his pillow. At first he thought it was Hilda trying to reach him from her secret retreat in the swamp. It wasn't her voice, though. This was a voice arriving from a greater distance. Freddie could hear the rumbling of thunder followed by an increasing noise level in his ears. He assumed he was suffering from his usual tinnitus, a maddening condition caused by his playing drums in a rock band when he was in his teens.

Yet there was something more eerie going on in his ear canal than just the roaring. That solitary voice trying to reach him was meeting up with a cosmic pit bull of tornado force winds. After awhile it dawned on Freddie that Gabriel was trying to reach him. "What the hell do you want?" exclaimed Freddie, forgetting for a moment he was talking to the Lord's point man.

"Gabe, is that you? I am not receiving you." Freddie was beside himself. He couldn't believe that he was talking into his pillow. There was more interference; a cosmic storm of the first magnitude was distorting their communication. Gabriel's voice faded in the pillow, and nothing remained except dead air. Could he have imagined it all?

He figured that Hilda had put something in his evening hooch to induce an auditory hallucination. He turned in the direction where Cottonmouth was softly snoozing at a corner of the bed.

"Hey there, fellow, are you awake?" said Freddie, longing for a bit of small talk with his companion. Freddie, who couldn't stand to drink alone, would desperately summon Cottonmouth to join him for a nightcap, filling a tiny drinking bowl for his friend with a concoction he distilled in his grimy bathtub, unsuitable for consuming by either man or snake. As time went by, his bathtub began turning a deep oxide red, and the enamel started to chip off in blackened flakes.

This didn't seem to trouble Freddie but it sent a strong signal to his buddy to use caution before daring to nap in that tub. It was only later, when that rotgut potation wreaked havoc on his bowels, that Freddie ceased making his homemade spirits, which suited Cottonmouth just fine, especially as he enjoyed taking the odd midday nap in that bathtub. But his reptilian intuition would first kick in, warning him to slide his sniffing tongue along the interior of the tub first to see if there was any deleterious substance there that would prove injurious to his health. As for any obnoxious presences of Freddie, there were virtually none. Freddie scarcely ever bathed.

A Talking Snake

Cottonmouth uncoiled at the sound of Freddie's voice. A shiver of revulsion swept through his elasticized body. He so desperately needed his restorative twelve hours sleep, and would have lunged out at Freddie had he not been so tired. It would have proved futile to sink his fangs into Freddie, who would mistake the perforations for a sign of affection; as did Hilda who enjoyed the odd nip in the back of her neck, on her thighs, a fast bite above or below the Venus mound, or a chaw aimed straight at the buttock.

Hilda was intrigued with sex in the wild, and often ogled pairs of grunting feral hogs springing into action. So impressed was she with that heat which engaged uninhibited feral swinery that she decided to investigate the possibility of gratifying the rutting need of any male striped boar searching for a quick fix in a Florida bog. Freddie groaned into his pillow. He was dreaming he was being ingurgitated by quicksand and yelping for help.

Just as it seemed the quicksand would engulf him, he woke with a jolt. Cottonmouth had lassoed Freddie's legs together and was attempting to pull him off his bed. "I've had it with you," hissed Cottonmouth. Freddie barely managed to get the words out of his mouth: "A talking snake, I can't believe it, no, it can't be, that's it – I am still dreaming." Cottonmouth directed a vibratory tongue at Freddie. "Believe it, you piece of frog turd!"

Cottonmouth's pupils were seared with fiery detestation. "Move over," he squalled, "stop hogging my side of the bed. I need room to stretch. Can't you see my body needs to lengthen? So pull over to your side of the bed!" He would have done more in the way of damage if Freddie hadn't offered that testy viper more territorial access to the bed they shared. This concession pleased Cottonmouth, for he stopped trying to yank Freddie, thereby giving him a chance to free his legs.

Freddie decided on a strategic retreat. Abandoning his bed, he dashed outside his dwelling where he picked up a musky odour, and in the lunar light followed what he discerned to be a scent trail where he found Hilda lustfully enveloped in the embrace of some dark furry being.

Porco Pete

How it dismayed Freddie to find his darling in the arms of a stranger who, upon closer inspection, turned out to be a feral boar, a tusky warrior. In an instant, this fiend would charge and disembowel an adversary. Porco Pete, as he was known to the locals, had taken refuge in Freddie's neighbourhood.

The snorty beast, he reckoned, had he been felled by a hunter, would have made a treasury of what seemed an endless supply of pulled pork. Yessie had tried and failed to bag what he dim-wittedly surmised to be a thousand pound porker. The porcine critter got larger each time Yessie and other swampbillys came across him. Loose and quick on the trotter, the beast had bolted into the sycamore woods surrounding the marshland.

Yessie had tried to follow Porco Pete, and in his haste stepped into a bog hole. Hearing the suction below his feet, and caught up in a panic, he swam fast in the direction of what he saw as solid ground, grateful to escape perilous quicksand!

Freddie alone gazed at that entwined couple, then turned away from this disturbing sight, heading home to be with Cottonmouth. His pal suffered separation anxiety. When left alone in the cabin, Cottonmouth trashed the place, knocked over dishes and made a revolting mess, venting his feelings of abandonment.

Freddie viewed the matter as a mere temper tantrum of any toddler during the terrible twos. To assuage Cottonmouth's distress, Freddie would pour some of his specially fermented buttermilk into a tiny bowl, taking pleasure in viewing his sidekick lapping up the foul-smelling concoction with that lapping tongue, which often delighted Hilda.

Now Freddie was up for making small talk, in expectation that his bedmate would enjoy his prattle before they both crashed into bed. Cottonmouth, however, wasn't into chit chat. He was getting drowsy.

"You piece of rotting skunk cabbage," he hissed venomously. "Damn you. Shut your hole! I need my sleep!" With that admonishment, he slid off the bed onto the floor, coiled into his usual ball and slept like a newborn kitten.

A Special Kind of Reptile

It was all an aberration, thought Freddie: snakes don't talk. They just hiss and piss and not much more than that. He began to suspect that Hilda had spiked his usual evening drink. Snakes have no voices, Freddie kept telling himself, as he stared into the washroom mirror and studied his complexion carefully – and even if Cottonmouth was a special kind of reptile, it didn't mean he could speak English; maybe Korean .

"That's a load of croc shit," exclaimed Yessie, with a twitch in his right eye when Freddie raised the matter of Cottonmouth's cussing in English. Yessie cautioned Freddie not to say a damned thing to others in the neighbourhood else they would think he was cultivating illicit weed for the purpose of trafficking. "Zip your trap!" declared Yessie with a more pronounced twitch, exposing a blood line in his retinal vein. "You're going to end up on some cashew farm with the other nut cases."

Freddie shrugged. "Maybe he's speaking Korean?"

Yessie had one endearing feature – a deep concern for his friend's well-being, coupled with an irrepressible loathing for Hilda. At the very mention of her name, a seismic wave of raw expletives flew out of his mouth. He warned Freddie to drop the "swamp bitch, she's a no-good Jezebel," and then, in the very next breath, raised the matter again of Freddie selling him Cottonmouth, which Freddie adamantly refused, brushing aside his offer as he would a biting midge landing on his arm. There was no way Cottonmouth was going to become a stretchable belt or some fancy patterned neckwear for anyone. Freddie wouldn't admit his perverse delight to Yessie that he enjoyed the way Cottonmouth gripped Hilda's dildo firmly between his jaws, dragging it along the floor and then slithering up onto the bed, dropping the dildo beside Hilda, grunting and wheezing like a rutting weasel.

Every Bit the Rocker

There was no way he would sell a damned talented snake, one with the potential to draw tourists. They would lay down some serious money to see his pal play fetch with a dildo under some big tent! But if Cottonmouth really talked, any voluble blather would do. Freddie envisioned a choreographed Cottonmouth on centre stage, a deep rose light bathing his lengthening body while he emitted a highly vocalized slam dunk of a Pentecostal "speaking in tongues" performance.

Even if the crowd, in the main, were non-believers, and didn't have a clue as to what Cottonmouth was actually vocalizing, it making no linguistic sense, except possibly to some backwater sect, the multitude would still be enthralled. Dead or living amphibians would be tossed on the stage in lieu of scented fresh-cut flowers; an adoring audience would leap to its feet and applaud.

Cottonmouth would feel those accolades vibrating under his shingled skin. Gratefully he would reciprocate with an extended hissing, shaking and rocking as though possessed by the spirit of the great Elvis, the difference being that poor disadvantaged Cottonmouth had no hips. Nevertheless, despite his handicap, Cottonmouth was every bit the rocker.

He surely would have brought down the house if he had possessed a developed derrière and flexible hips to grind and round out the beat. Entertaining a dream of building a global entertainment empire by exploiting hipless Cottonmouth, Freddie had failed to notice Yessie was derisively eyeballing him, a gaze made all the more pronounced by nervous facial tics, which made both his eyes twitch. It was a transient neurological disorder that ran in Yessie's family; his father having had the condition, and upon surrendering his mortal coils, his twitching eyes tried to make eye contact with his Maker just as a vortex of dark air snatched his soul and conveyed it below the earth's crust to the Lake of Fire.

The Cussing Disease

Yessie had also inherited a mild form of Tourette's syndrome, a cussing disorder, but learned to mask it by distorting that all-purpose adjectival currency of the rough house crowd, muffling the F word, and stretching it to the elastic limit. Yessie had learned to say "ffffffffffffruck this" and "ffffffffffffruck that." His affliction would combust when something irked him, such as Freddie broaching the matter of his involvement with Hilda.

"You're crazier than an outhouse rat on steroids," yawped Yessie. "You and your whore are heading straight to hell. Yep, Old Sulfur is ffffffffrucken waiting for you. Frucccccck it, I can hear the ffffffffffrucken flames crackling, laughing for the likes of you fornicating rapscallions, you'll both sizzle well. Best you sell me that dirty ffffffffffffffffffffrucken snake right ffffffffffffffrucken now."

Freddie was about to lambaste his annoying friend and give him a good tongue lashing, when Yessie's neurological state went seismic, involuntary twitches strayed from the lower reaches of his face and crawled upward like a sportive insect. Then Freddie made a phenomenal discovery: a barely detectable incandescence issued from what he discerned to be some ophthalmic seedling directly embedded in the centre of Yessie's forehead.

Had Yessie noticed that he was in possession of a third eye, he may well have decided it was a sinful eye, generally transmitted by Satan to absorb the sight of relentless fornication.

Yessie's excessive Biblical ingurgitation would have immediately red-flagged Matthew 18:9 (King James Bible – *And if thine eye offend thee, pluck it out, and cast it from thee: it is better for thee to enter into life with one eye, rather than having two eyes to be cast into hellfire*).

Fortunately for that teensy visual organ, Yessie kept no mirrors in his dwelling, and so this precious ophthalmic seedling had never yet been outed. Or plucked!

The Lilliputian Peeper

The more cognizant Freddie became of Yessie's cryptic eye, the more agitated his thoughts were, swarming as they began gorging on the more diminutive cogitation until a bubbling thought, one more opaque than the others, queried whether that infinitesimal eye was merely a decorative ornament, or a ghost roving about in the Stygian darkness of Yessie's psyche. Freddie studied the Lilliputian peeper.

He wondered if Yessie was an evolving reptile. There was something in Yessie's icy visage which reminded him of Cotton-mouth's calculating deportment, summed up in a brittle smile moments before ingurgitating a live mouse, food that s*chmecks* to a famished viper.

"What the fffffffffffffruck, are you ffffffrucking looking at?" Yessie suddenly blurted, unnerved by Freddie's intense gaze which came to rest on the clandestine itsy-bitsy eye. Yessie kept mangling the F word, fearing if he didn't blur the word he would be deep-fried in the Lake of Fire. The miniscule rogue eye fiercely outshone Yessie's two other *über* eyes.

What Yessie couldn't see, though, he couldn't pluck out.

Lucy

Yessie experienced recurring nightmares. Some evenings he would awaken to find that his entire body was lathered in sweat, and then fear took hold as he began to imagine he was a dead man. There was a familiar smell in his bedroom, a heady odour similar to that of decomposing octopus stinkhorn, a bizarrely shaped fungus, often referred to by the locals as "dead man's fingers," for its gruesome shape, that of curved pinkish red fingers imprisoned within a fruited body that attracts amorous green bottle flies.

His macabre olfactory experience left him drained, and it took him awhile to realize he was among the living, unlike his favourite bloodhound Jack, a bossy although affectionate dog with aristocratic airs, who had been fried by lightning during a nasty thunderstorm.

Laved in a broth of the same perspiration was Yessie's itsy-bitsy eye, which Freddie had nicknamed Lucy, for there was a distinctive familiarity to that diminutive peeper. Freddie had met Yessie's mother Lucy at church and community functions. She often showed her disapproval of Yessie's women that he was courting and yearned to marry.

There was never a woman good enough for her boy, and Yessie, ever challenged in his powers of deduction, failed to realize his mother, being widowed when Yessie was still a youngster, wanted him all to herself, taking comfort that there was "a man about the house" to see to her well-being and to read the Bible to her most evenings as her eyesight was failing.

She owned him outright with her scraggy skin and sclerotic hands that complemented her narrow agate eyes, always swelling with righteous anger. As punishment for challenging her suzerainty, she would force a Jesus drink on him. He grimaced in disgust, his eyes twitching as he raised a nipperkin of gall laced with wine vinegar to his lips, and began to realize why the King of Kings had the good sense to refuse that Golgotha highball offered by the sadistic Roman guards at his Crucifixion.

"No, Momma...no!" Yessie would protest, gently pushing her away, but his mother's eye glommed onto him, turning his will into mouse jelly. Raising his sight skyward, and hoping for the best, he slowly drank the abomination, and after a while, to his amazement, he took a shine to his mother's mixology. She could have run a bar service for Satan.

Control Freak

Mercifully for Yessie, Lucy had passed into the spirit world at a hundred and four and a good thing too, for she was contemplating adding bat guano to her fabulous potion to give it the right "martyr's bouquet."

Desiring to get to know Yessie better, the principia maternal in Lucy craved an outer and inner intimacy with him, for if she could share his sweat, then why not a dream or two? There was another flawed personality feature to this alien seedling of an eye; Lucy didn't care to share Yessie with his other two eyes. Lucy, without a doubt, had a nasty jealous side and she lived on in Yessie's pipsqueak eye as an imperious spirit, what in contemporary parlance is known as a "control freak."

Each time Freddie met Yessie he noted a subtle change in his subversive eye. A puzzling morphization was taking place in his seedling eye: it was less feline, more human, and changeable in colour, shifting from emerald to teal, even to obsidian at will, which meant the First Lady, the dowager Lucy, was running the show and that Yessie's mother would always have something to bleat about his love life, dead or not.

A month after his mother's passing, he found himself afflicted by a desire to wear his momma's clothes and roll around in bed murmuring praises to her, hoping the adoration would not get lost in some dead letter office in deep space, but continue en route to the open call box by the Pearly Gates.

So long as the wicked seedling eye existed, Yessie would never be free of Lucy. Indeed, so overwhelming was her dominance, he would find himself continually resisting a compulsion to go drag in Lucy's best finery, especially the Sunday duds that she wore to church: her flowered frock with its sleek velour collar, white dimity blouse and lambskin gloves. He was particularly attracted to his mother's shimmering black leather pumps.

He would polish those shoes until they shone with an oily glaze. It made them more compelling, idolatrously attractive to his perverse, guilt-nibbled mind.

Lurking Lucy

There was one particular version of a dream which any metamorphosed variant of Lucy was determined to etherealize. For Yessie it was the crème de la crème of dreams, as in it Hilda was finally tamed and completely under Yessie's authority.

She played out the reverie as a cringing slave, submissive to his every command in or out of bed. Lucy, a despoiler of dreams, knew that, besides his lusting after Hilda, what really turned his sundial was a fondness for young impressionable nurses, preferably those in training, whose psyches he considered moldable as plasticine, readily twisted to gratify his deepest sexual urges.

Lucy didn't care if the sexual congress with a "nursie" took place in some intangible dream cocoon, which she couldn't witness, or outside the dream where she could frightfully ogle the pair copulating.

In truth, Lucy, in any femme mineralization, had never much cared for threesomes, even if all she could do was play the role of a Peeping Jane in the guise of a miniscule twitchy third party eye. Had she a reversible power to stare into the boudoir of some dream of his, scrumptiously pornographic in all its lewd minutiae, she would have mustered a full whammy and in a jealous rage vaporized it.

Yessie would have awoken the following morning, the baffled owner of an erection, and feeling all the more flustered, since he couldn't establish the source of his tumescent affliction in the real world and in his own true rumpled and soiled bed. All he could do then, suspecting he had guiltily committed an act of self-love, was consult his well-fingered Bible, and pour over Genesis 38:9 (English Standard Version 2001):

"But Onan knew that the offspring would not be his. So whenever he went in to his brother's wife he would waste the semen on the ground, so as not to give offspring to his brother."

There was no way of escaping his mother. Like a feral cat desperate for the taste of a freshly killed goldfinch, Lucy was out there lurking around, ready to pounce and devour every sinew of Yessie's spiritual envelope, leaving nothing for other demons to chew, not even an ectoplasmic beak.

Mirrors

Having no mirrors in his dwelling to reflect that speck of a third eye back to his other two über eyes, there was no way for Yessie to discover he possessed a rogue eye. Neither Freddie nor Hilda cared to inform Yessie of his arcane eye, and as for Cottonmouth, he stayed clear of Yessie, fearing him and his freakish orb, which never failed to glare menacingly at Cottonmouth, filling him with such seismic terror that he felt his skin would prematurely slough off. After that, the one calming moment for Cottonmouth was to meticulously study his own image in a mirror. It seemed to suggest that he yearned to reconnect with some lost essence, even if his keeper didn't believe a snake could possibly possess a soul.

Unlike Yessie, who eschewed mirrors, believing the devil dwelt within their fused silica properties, luring the gullible along a lustrous pathway to evil doing, Cottonmouth enjoyed the company of mirrors. He never missed an opportunity to cast a few furtive glances at the bathroom mirror while Freddie was shaving. Freddie, seeing Cottonmouth reflected in the background, sensed that his live-in companion appeared famished for more self-reflection, so he moved to one side of the mirror, gesturing to him to slither forward and get the full whammy of glassy sustenance. Freddie's offer was refused.

Living Food

How Cottonmouth wished that the scales on his body were as reflective as a mirror; for then he could both attract and mesmerize his quarry, all for a slow gut-busting meal. In his own way he was praising the current dining-out crowd of "foodies," and exalting their views on "slow food," in contrast to loveless "fast food" served up at a local burger joint.

Nothing could be more organic for Cottonmouth than chowing down on natural living *food*, as in sucking up a *free-range rodent*, and at such a gradual pace that any onlooker witnessing the gastric action would fall asleep long before the rat's vibrating tail passed through the gateway of his gaping white mouth.

A Mother Is Always a Mother

Cottonmouth had good reason to steer clear of Yessie. It wasn't solely because he feared Yessie's cryptic eye, but he was more perturbed by Yessie's aggressive offers to purchase him for top money and turn him into a luxuriously patterned belt, or, if there was enough snakish material left over, a matching tie sartorially distinctive, if a tad on the flashy side, for Yessie to wear to church on Sunday.

A green-hued incandescence in Cottonmouth's peepers suddenly froze, stunned into a glaciated submission by the memory of Yessie's teensy eye. It reminded him of his mother's disapproval when he refused to share a half-regurgitated swamp rat with the rest of the family brood, a younger brother and several sisters. On that occasion she vented her anger, telling him that she wished he was a stillborn meal for some egg-sucking weasel!

His mother's deprecation of him only ended when she was snatched up by a gator while lazily sunning herself on a patch of dry ground. Cottonmouth, who, had witnessed his mother's violent demise, would go on to suffer a post-traumatic stress peculiar to reptiles, undulating and nocturnally wetting the bed he shared with Freddie. Cottonmouth's mother, while she was alive, had never warmed up to him in a huggy way, yet he continued to grieve her passing, reasoning that *a mother is always a mother*, whether kind, cruel or indifferent.

One does not ask to be popped through the shell of an egg. It just happens. Cottonmouth was more fortunate than Yessie. At least he was free of an itsy-bitsy additional eye and its occupant, a demonoid mother.

A Trivial Earthly Matter

"I think Mother is trying to reach me," said Yessie wistfully, trepidation rattling in his voice box. Freddie, in a vain attempt to calm his friend down, tried explaining to Yessie that he, himself, had undergone some unnatural communication by way of his pillow, and that it was perfectly natural to talk into one's pillow to receive messages from a higher and more ennobled source somewhere in deep space.

Freddie became more disquieted each time Yessie broached the topic of his mother. He surmised that she got her jollies by cussing out Yessie, and sensed that she would have gone on to poison his soul by her toxic utterances, if at the right moment an unseen power greater than her own hadn't put up a protective vapour barrier between her and Yessie.

Her favourite reproach to Yessie could have been scripted in a *Mommy Dearest* movie, as with that insane harridan, Joan Crawford, Lucy was at her cinematic best venting her spleen at her dullard son.

"You piece of trash, I should have aborted you. You're disgusting!" Her invective reverberated in Yessie's ears, turning him into the emotional equivalent of a putrefying swamp otter swarmed by a cloud of obese flies in bombilation. Her tirade against him brought on the mulligrubs. It enveloped him in a cobalt blue vapour, and yet still he followed the dictates of the Good Book, Ephesians 6:1-3, and continued loving Lucy.

To Freddie, it appeared that Yessie's bond to his mother was indestructible, glued together by what he perceived to be the craziest mucilage in the universe. Something had to be done to free Yessie. He thought of contacting Gabriel, seeking his help to unglue Yessie from his mother. But would Gabriel respond to Freddie's plea? Freddie began to have his doubts: as messenger Numero Uno, Gabriel was on overload delivering his Master's warnings to hirsute evildoers in sinful cities, towns, villages and hamlets, and consequently, he wasn't so readily available to deal with such a trivial earthly matter as expelling Lucy's malignant presence tucked away in his third eye. Freddie's use of the moniker, "Gabe," as Freddie was wont to address Gabriel, shocked the other angels. Nicknames were an affront to these messengers of the Lord, who expected to be properly addressed by their given name. Freddie's insensitivity set off a rippling protest of celestial wings, so powerful as to set a slumbering cloud adrift in a cerulean blue sky.

The angelic fraternity considered Freddie little more than an impure being, formed from rodent feces. Freddie had no idea he was held in such contempt by those messengers of brightness. In any case he sensed that Gabe couldn't be counted on to decimate Lucy. So Freddie resolved to find another way to snuff her out.

He contemplated gouging out the offending nipper eye, when next Yessie crashed from too much drink, for the two layabouts often sought to drink each other under the table, with a thoroughly besotted Yessie ending up the loser, his pants awash in piss.

Freddie would seize the opportune moment when Yessie was anesthetized on cheap gin, and scoop out that indefatigable vision seed with a nifty silver-plated teaspoon. (He usually used this family heirloom to feed another object of his affection – a carnivorous pitcher plant – conveying generous tidbits of ripened hamburger meat to his insectivorous pet.)

Now another option came dimly into view: Cottonmouth's fangs seemed especially made for a lightning surgical nip, and presto – the puny eye would be neatly extracted along with a septic discharge of devilry of all that was Lucy, who then would be rendered as helpless as a newborn lamb in a sheepfold, fixed upon by the citrine lights of a drooling wolf.

Freddie's pillow was occupied by Cottonmouth. His sinister head turned in Freddie's direction, his split tongue vibrating as he spoke.

"She's seeing that oinker tonight; the bitch is two-timing you again."

"I need the pillow," said Freddie, awestruck that he was confronted once again by a reptile with a penchant for salty language.

"She's a no-good hussy," sibilated Cottonmouth. Freddie rubbed his ears. He couldn't believe what he was hearing.

"I'm not moving, and all your candy-ass bullshit won't work its charm on me." For good measure, to make his point, he lashed the tip of his tail at Freddie.

"I have to get an urgent message off to Gabe," said Freddie meekly.

"You don't mean fluff boy or is it fluffy girl?" snickered Cottonmouth, ejecting an impressive gob of vitriol directly at the pillow.

It landed precisely on the spot where Freddie's right ear would have normally rested while waiting for an incoming message from Gabe. Cottonmouth slithered off the pillow, turned momentarily in Freddie's direction, and hissed, "Ssssee you around, sssssucker."

Death Fix

It was long after Freddie's failed attempt to reach Gabriel that Cottonmouth began pressing his head into a corner of Freddie's pillow, hissing and salivating into Freddie's left ear. While this wasn't the pillow etiquette he had come to expect from Cottonmouth, it was only later that Freddie realized just how fortunate he was, for if he hadn't extracted Cottonmouth's venom the previous morning, he would have ended up as stiff as the cheap clapboard he used for the mildewed walls of his dwelling.

It left Freddie musing what the ultimate rush would have felt like *had he forgotten to milk his companion's venom on the previous morning.* That death fix trigged a peculiar fantasy: it left him wondering who would turn up at his funeral and what unflattering conversations would transpire among the mourners, while he lay at rest in an open walnut box with a blue velvet interior, clad in the Armani suit he could never afford while he was alive.

Staring into the open casket, a black ribbon attached firmly to his neck, a grief-stricken Cottonmouth would be shedding tears.

Freddie suddenly awoke, startled, but relieved he was still among the living. Cottonmouth's lidless peepers sparkled with mischief. Freddie, to be sure he wasn't still dreaming, lightly slapped both sides of his face, which triggered an inspired response from Cottonmouth. Thinking this was Freddie's way of requesting some rough trade, he deftly aimed his elasticized tail against both sides of Freddie's face, cheeks, raising purplish welts. Always the artful perfectionist, Cottonmouth leaned back from his portion of the pillow to admire the view and, if snakes could be said to smile, his smile was so tight, it yanked in the corners of his mouth.

Little Boy

Freddie yearned to free his beloved Hilda from Porco, being especially on his guard against the thrusts of that beast's razor-sharp
tusks. He knew that Porco had once charged a swampbilly before
he could empty his Browning BPS 12-gauge shotgun into the
snorting beast to dispatch him.

In a matter of seconds, Porco's pointy tusks had gone straight
through the man's chest, ripping out his heart, launching it into the
air in a fountain of blood, squishing it with an ungulate's fury. That
hunter had intended to show off his peccary trophy to his hairy
gator hunting pals, maybe inviting them to try out his specialty, his
barbequed double-smoked pulled pork; alas, he had scuppered his
chance of bringing home a monumental free-range hoofer, whose
head, mounted on his wall, would have made a wonderful conversation piece.

Feral pigs will gorge on anything they can get their snouts into,
from larvae, rodents and mushrooms, to native plants, frogs and
even nesting birds on the ground. Nevertheless, a hoofer like Porco
can discover he has a charitable soft spot when he leaves a portion
of a vanquished adversary behind for other famished swamp
lodgers, before retreating from the zone of combat with an unkiss-
able smile cracking his disdainful lips.

Subsequently, a snappish alligator, cascading sprays of brackish water, his mouth agape, the cavities of his nostrils sucking air
– and with his webbed forelimbs and hind limbs planted firmly on
the mud flat – secures Porco's gift, while tears surge from the corners of his eyes. As Fate would later have it, some gator hunters,
having whacked a snarly gator and cut open the reptile's scaly
white belly, were horrified to find a partially eaten head, a water-
proofed insulated rubber swamp boot, along with the ragged
remains of a monogrammed US grey army fatigue shirt spelling
out the victim's initials, ML, for Mutt Lafarge, known to the serial

gator-killing community as "Little Boy," who was a lean and mean seven footer, two ax handles in breadth across the shoulders below a gigantic head.

Suffering from gigantism, his head, when it was attached to his body, seemed smaller and grossly out of proportion with the rest of his frame. DNA would later confirm that this head belonged to Mutt, the very man who had promised his beer-sozzled friends that he would blow away "the biggest damned hoofer this side of heaven." And yet a further mystery remained: why wasn't that expensive shotgun ever found?

Cottonmouth, having witnessed the deadly action between the two warriors, thought it wise to stay clear of Porco, knowing his fondness for devouring snakes. Yet, now in a conjugal dream, there he was, being led on a short dog leash by Freddie. He didn't much care to play the role of a servile pet, not for Freddie anyway. For Hilda, however, tender inklings were beginning to overtake him to the point where he could imagine a leash of hers sweetly tethering his serpentine throat.

A Moss Pit of Their Own

In a conjoined dream, Freddie and Cottonmouth follow a pathway in a bog illuminated by rising columns of burning methane. Dazzled by the spook lights flickering to the beating of distant drums, the pair are filled with apprehension as they arrive at an opening in the marsh to witness a spectacle of swamp people dressed in gator skins, thrusting their fists in the air, kicking and jabbing, as in some roughshod ballet. These pear-shaped gator-hunting home boys (and a few burly gals) thunder their heavy gumboots until the muddy ground rumbles.

None of the assembled would ever have been caught dead in tights, leaping gracefully into the air in dainty slippers, but they were especially contemptuous of urban moshers and their mosh pit hooplas, preferring instead to rock in their own "moss pit," formed on spongy patches of mossy ground in some herbaceous bog.

A tuned-in onlooker viewing their tribal ritual might have assumed some aberrant spirit was loose among the assemblage, with each performer invoking an incantation in what sounded like humming and clacking insect-like noises to the rhythm of beating drums in the background.

Freddie and Cottonmouth were in awe of the intense performance with the latter undulating in applause, jetting his vibratory tongue gustily out of his cottony white mouth, which, to his surprise, had turned stark titanium white, so taken was he with that ceremonial dance.

Yet, in applauding these performers, he had not taken into account that the squirrel-eating lot held other less ennobled values than tribal bonding. He may have prematurely sloughed off his skin to learn they were keen in supplying not just gator hide but viper integument to entrepreneurs engaging in a profitable high-end market in the manufacture of custom-made fetishized snakeskin leatherwear featuring cowboy boots, broad-brimmed Aussie

Outback banded hats, belts, purses, wallets and the *crème de la crème* – distinctively embossed ties appearing to wriggle in a clothes closet for the hard-core fashion plate who has it all.

Enter the Controller

Miraculously, there weren't any collisions of moss pit bodies as a long line of stomping and hand-flailing participants began forming a large primary circle, which then split apart, with the celebrants charging off in opposite directions to form frenzied circles within circles. Freddie and Cottonmouth, while enjoying the mossy floor show, wondered who called the shots for those ecstatic revellers.

It didn't take long for them to discover who their controller was, for when the drumming suddenly ceased, a towering figure of a swampbilly appeared. His bulging battleship-grey eyes made his fearful presence known to the mossers.

A gator hoody swept over the ridge of his crooked nose which tended to wobble, indicating that his beak had been broken numerous times in dust-ups with rogue mossers who challenged his authority.

He took a little pride in knowing his defective schnoz served as a three-dimensional warning logo: to steer clear of him. And he had other brutish features to enrich his bestial nature: there was a furry wildlife element realized in his full beard topiary, so plentiful in his salt and pepper hair, that had it been properly cut, harvested, and mucilaged to leafage and twigs, there would have been enough bristly material to create a capacious swallow's nest in some abandoned barn.

That tonsorial-defying beard seemed to have a will all its own. Climbing downward over his beer-swollen potbelly, his beard animated each time he fired off a barrage of configurative dance directions over the heads of the gator-clad crowd who, before going into their dance number, responded in what sounded to Freddie like a chorus of garburated hosannas. An enthralled Cottonmouth, however, acknowledged their voluble joy with a flick of the far tip of his tail.

"Say, they're not going to sacrifice some virgin are they?" Freddie whispered. Freddie rubbed his forehead, perplexed at what he was witnessing. "Heck," he spat, "There're no virgins around here no more. Shit, they're scarcer than the golden limp-kins we used to see around these parts."

"Look," said Cottonmouth, suddenly wheezing like a sick marmot. "They got something in that big bag." And sure enough, the super canvas bag started moving, but just barely. Soon they heard a muffled squeal coming from inside the bag which Freddie took to be a body bag, the type used by homicide police teams for morbidly obese cadavers. Suddenly the drumming and dance ritual ceased and the moss pit boss stood menacingly before his mossy underlings, signalling for their rapt attention.

Porco Pete Smoked

"Listen up, you worthless mud-sucking bloodworms," cried the controller. Cackling and drooling into his beard, the saddle of his nose quivered as he slowly raised the bag to shoulder level, shaking it violently. "We got ourselves that hoofer who killed our buddy, Little Boy, Yes, siree."

"You don't mean that mean ass, tusky son of a bitch that some call Porco Pete?" an emboldened mosser cried out. "Yes, wormo," snapped the controller. There followed a massive clapping of hands and stomping of boots on the mossy ground. Some mossers could be heard calling for Porco to be whacked, gutted and served up as barbequed pulled pork.

Things finally came to a boil when the controller suddenly dropped the squirming bag and pulled out a six-shot Colt 2 Detective Special snub nose revolver from a shoulder holster under his hoody, opened the bag and aimed his firearm directly at the head of Porco, who thrashed about looking pleadingly at his executioner.

There was a collective hush in the air. Freddie held his breath, while Cottonmouth went into hyperventilations, hissing and burping gas, in dread over what was to follow.

"This is for Little Boy, you murdering fat bastard," raged the controller, firing a single shot and, in that instant, Porco Pete lay dead, piggy eyes chilled, staring skyward. A few of the more morbidly curious mossers proceeded over to the open bag to get a better view of the once dreaded Porco. And then, to the controller's complete surprise, one of the onlookers began admonishing him for ruining what would have been a perfect feral hog head to mount on a game room wall.

Why didn't the shooter aim instead at Porco's massive chest to dispatch him?

"Shut your hole, damn you," growled the controller, holstering the Colt. "Big deal," he guffawed, with a vehement shake of his fist.

"Lookee here, maggot. So there's a hole in his head, that's even better. Means it's one hell of a conversation piece. I say just wash up the blood around that hole, and yeah, leave the bullet tucked inside."

The question now remained: who would get Porco's head, even if it wasn't in mint condition? Could they hold a draw? The controller was vexed at that suggestion. There would be no draw. Porco's head was his to mount alongside the other trophies on his dining-room wall. His head would be a perfect match mounted next to a huge gator head he called "Corky." "Boys," declared the controller, allowing a little drool to slide from a corner of his mouth, "I say we remember Little Boy when we next chow down on this hoofer."

Soon a lively banter began among the mossers: who would do the butchering, what smoker would they to use, given a choice between a wood, an electric, or even a gas grill smoker, and for the actual smoking process, would it be sugar maple wood chunks or chips?

Cottonmouth's heart began to beat faster than usual; for with Porco out of the equation, only Freddie remained as his rival for Hilda's affection. "Time to blow out of here," whispered Freddie. Cottonmouth, reflecting on Porco's fate, suppressed an inward glee as they headed home on a pathway brightened by ghostly light flaring from rising will-o'-the-wisps haunting the night.

The following morning Cottonmouth awoke and slithered off the bed. Freddie was still asleep but it was a troubled sleep, for he kept moaning aloud for Porco's life to be spared.

Cottonmouth didn't care much for dreams, reasoning that if you couldn't smell, taste or gorge on a dream, relishing it like a slow-food eater devouring newborn ducklings abandoned in a nest by their mother, then what use were dreams?

Eternal Glue

A short time after Porco Pete was murdered by the moss pit controller, Cottonmouth started behaving erratically. It began with a flood of fabrications, so outrageous that Freddie thought that Cottonmouth was undergoing a nervous breakdown.

Little Boy's head, Cottonmouth paranoically declared, spiking his revelation with more than the usual sarcasm, was mounted on the controller's game room wall next to the damaged head of Porco Pete.

Again bewildered by a talking reptile, Freddie wondered if some malignant force had entered his noggin to play the ventriloquist using his chum as a dummy mouthpiece.

In truth, Mutt Lafarge's head had been retrieved from a gator's gut and placed in an ice chip filled cooler, and then rushed over to the district pathologist Thomas Shuttlecock Melon, who hurriedly and generously applied a combo of antibiotic and antifungal cream to prevent the onslaught of skin necrosis on Mutt's face.

Had Mutt's head rested another day entombed inside the gator, there would have been nothing to preserve of Mutt's features. At least, this was Dr. Melon's opinion.

Known as "Melon Head" by friend and foe alike, he also functioned as an innovative funeral director at a mortuary in the nearby metropolis of Gorgonia. Often the pressures of his job would take its toll, for he would find himself bubbling with laughter in the company of close friends, and he would giddily refer to himself as the Death King.

Yet paradoxically, while he relished his grim moniker, he couldn't bear it when some lout addressed him as Melon Head. In an instant he would be transformed from the doughy, mild-mannered mortician that he was, into the snarling personality of some gator about to steamroll a vacationing family's beloved poodle.

Later, Mutt's head itself was placed in a large ceramic container to be thoroughly laved in a brew of formaldehyde, embalming glycerin, pickling spices (used in preserving pastrami and corned beef), magnesium zinc salts, Hawaiian queen bee jelly, super pasteurized honey, clear flowing beeswax, salicylic acid, and further garnished with a lime and papaya extract, rich in vitamins and antioxidants, not to mention active enzymes to thwart cellular damage.

If this wasn't enough in the way of creative wizardry, that monstrous soup was further embellished with zesty additives known to the ancient pharaonic embalmers, and passed onto the skin biologists and chemists employed in that funeral establishment.

Laura née Dewberry a cosmetic artist, went to work on Mutt's face. Eye candy to a few of the gator jocks, she ignored their vicious taunts that she was getting it on with the cadavers she was charged to make more presentable. Significant painterly skills were required to get the job done right, and it could be said she displayed the attributes of a meticulous and inventive landscape painter, although one using the topological flesh of the departed as a canvas.

But if she had her share of verbal abuse from a few lugs in the gator-killing fraternity, she also had her admirers. Some of Mutt's friends swore that in death their chum looked better than when he was alive. They couldn't help but note the robust colour restored to his cheeks.

With friends and family members in attendance, and Yessie as lay pastor from the Church of Yeshua the Redeemer, delivering the last of the lines in Psalm 23:4 at Mutt's open grave, Mutt's head was gently placed in a vacuum-sealed bell jar, the jar lid sealed shut by a special epoxy trademarked Eternal Glue.

Bewailed by mourners, his head entombed in a jar, Mutt was laid to rest for all eternity under the sacred mossy ground of the Joyous Elysian Fields cemetery.

What struck Freddie as awe-inspiring was the beatific smile on Mutt's lips before he was placed in that space-age sarcophagus. He couldn't heap enough praise on Laura's ingenuity. Didn't Melon Head realize he had a major artist in his employ?

Slow Food

To top up the fetid discharge of lies that swept toward Freddie, Cottonmouth suggested that a Porco Pete look-alike had been executed by the controller. The real "PP," as Cottonmouth was wont to call him, was still carousing with Hilda. "She's a two-timing sssssssssssssslut," hissed Cottonmouth, enjoying the snaky consonant.

Freddie rubbed his earlobe. He couldn't believe what he was hearing. "Porco Pete is certifiably 100 percent dead," replied Freddie testily, "and, little buddy, now don't you give me the hooey about a DNA match either."

Staring deeply into Cottonmouth's eyes, he wondered what other lies lay entombed alive inside his poisonous brain. Pitifully, just as a parent would try to explain the basics of life to a child, he told Cottonmouth that he had attended a mossers' barbeque and had witnessed PP being cut up into small portions, and cooked to perfection on a gas grill by none other than the controller himself, a blue-ribbon winning grill master, who made doubly sure that pieces of PP didn't taste like the bottom of an ashtray.

"You scum-sucking dudes ate the DNA evidence, damn you!" Cottonmouth gusted. Freddie chuckled, relishing the thought of having chowed down on Hilda's lover. "He tasted just scrumptious, but, hey, little buddy – maybe he was a bit over-smoked in places. Hickory isn't the best wood for smokin'. I prefer maple myself."

Cottonmouth found Freddie's gustatory preferences obscene, and he couldn't stand being addressed as "little buddy" when he was one huge stretchable buddy. The sight of Freddie eating dead meat made him feel nauseous.

It seemed so gastronomically perverse in contrast to dining on a struggling swamp rat, an all-day dining experience. It was at such slow foodie moments, his thoughts went astray.

He began envisioning a more challenging prey, devouring Gabriel, for instance, feathers and all. It made his pepsins bubble just to think how long it would take to turn him into liquid nourishment. And while his taste buds detected no protein in Gabriel, his loathing for the archangel provided a wonderful stimulant for an insatiable appetite, much like a one-handed matador vengefully plunging a fork into a tenderized steak from the very bull who gored him – thus ending what promised to be a meteoric career in the bullring.

Loathing can also be viewed as an antipasto platter of meaty tidbits leading up to the *pièce de résistance* of a main meal. *Bon appétit,* slow eaters!

Fetching

Now, it wasn't too long after Freddie had bested his "little buddy" that he noted some odd unsnakelike behaviour in Cottonmouth. He began to spew out lies, rampant poisonous bile. It first started with a string of obscene pillow calls to Gabriel, after which each time a call was placed to Gabriel from Freddie's soiled pillow, the line went unanswered. It wasn't too long after that Cottonmouth related to Freddie that he had been abducted when he'd taken a wrong turn in one of their conjoined dreams.

Somehow, in the small hours of the morning, he ended up at Dr. Melon's funeral establishment where he observed Laura birching the doctor's exposed alabaster white fanny.

"And then what happened, little buddy?" interjected Freddie, while rubbing his forehead and mumbling, "I'm cursed! This can't be happening to me."

Glaring menacingly at Freddie, Cottonmouth began dramatizing Laura's birching techniques by using the tip of his tail to simulate the vibratory rhythm of a whip setting off to target an imaginary derriere. Freddie's face quickly paled like a lump of freshly made dough ready to be slapped down to serve as a pizza crust.

Words dropped back into Freddie's frozen mouth. But Cottonmouth had already anticipated what Freddie would ask.

"She had me fetching her whip!" he sputtered.

Bruce

Although Cottonmouth's keen chemosensory system discerned enough snake in Hilda to gratify him, it galled him to have to share her with Freddie and other bog habitués, and gradually his jealousy transformed him into a rip-and-tear berserker. At first he vented his anger by nipping the tip of his tail, and for a while it seemed to dissipate his fury, but this was not to last, and a spark of anger reignited his rage. He had to strike out at something to vent his fury. It was either that or self-destruct.

Hissing, he slithered into the clothes closet to pick a fight with Freddie's collection of priceless ties, not only trashing the sleepy lot, the lesser snakish neckwear, but going out of his way by making an example of "Bruce," Freddie's favourite silken black tie, by shredding that *objet d'art*, which, in better days, had undulated to acknowledge Freddie as his master when he chose to wear Bruce on special occasions to match a grungy white shirt.

Still, it upset Bruce to think he could be in such close proximity to one so lacking in hygiene. What made Bruce endure the situation was the rapt attention he commanded of onlookers who met him for the first time. Gradually, even Freddie became aware of Bruce's strident attention seeking.

In part, Bruce's exhibitionist nature was boosted by Freddie's own enthused inclination to sport him at social engagements, with the expressed purpose of wowing impressionable young women, who couldn't resist an impulse to fondle Bruce, while at the same time, they feared coming in contact with Freddie's contaminated shirt, not to mention a musty odour redolent of decaying mould.

Freddie recalled how folks playing Bingo at the Gorgonia community hall had been bowled over by his hissing tie. It had proved quite the conversation-starter of a fashion item as people formed a line for the privilege of petting that slitherer, with one person even offering to trade his Rolex for Bruce. When Freddie discovered Cottonmouth's vicious acts of pillaging for revenge, nothing could dispel Freddie's grief over his loss. Months before, the passing of Snarlowe, his blind pit bull, had hit him hard. Snarlowe was a great fetcher; his only sin had been sniffing out some wash hanging on a neighbour's clothesline and getting shot for his curiosity. At heart, Snarlowe was a thief and a clever one.

Horrified at the loss of his alpha tie, Freddie resolved to get to the source of his companion's tantrum. This wasn't the placid mate, the compliant fetcher he thought he knew. Had the vigorous milker in Freddie gone too far in extracting Cottonmouth's venom? A snake professional was needed to examine Cottonmouth, and he knew exactly whom to consult.

Love Disease

"Just like I suspected – it's the dreaded *amor est mentis insani*," declared Dr. Ricardo Copperhead, the herpetologist in charge of the snake house at the Gorgonia zoo. Cottonmouth had contracted a potentially deadly malady known to the average layman as "the love disease." AEMI, to go by its acronym, had turned Freddie's usually passive companion into an aggressive brawler.

"Has your friend been in contact with, well, let me put it this way, with strumpets of his genus?"

"Who, what, genus?" blurted Freddie. Copperhead repressed a giggle and, noting the frightened look in Freddie's eyes, softly replied, "Has he been in contact with his own kind?" Freddie, puzzled by Copperhead's question, began to rub his forehead furiously as though massaging his memory.

"He doesn't stray too far from my house to cozy up to any strumpets of his – genus?" Catching his breath, Freddie became increasingly resentful of Copperhead's intrusiveness in enquiring of Cottonmouth's dalliances with some hottie of his "own kind." It flustered Freddie to think that his pal was on the prowl for some feminine affection, although it never once occurred to him that Hilda was the source of Cottonmouth's affliction.

"Now, Doc, what's all this hooey about love crapola?" Freddie's agitated state was unsettling Copperhead's cool demeanor.

"Calm yourself. Your friend's malady is very amenable to treatment."

Freddie looked directly into Copperhead's eyes. "You know, Doc, for a moment you had me thinking my little buddy caught some fatal dose."

"Oh yes, a dose," Copperhead snickered. "I assume you mean a sexually transmitted disease?"

"Yeah, a dose," said Freddie scornfully. "That's exactly what I mean."

"Not so," responded Copperhead with a now suave tone in his voice. "Let me assure you, your friend's affliction is quite treatable."

Copperhead realized he had to come up with some answers, and soon, for it appeared that Freddie was falling apart at the seams.

After palpating the length of his heavily sedated patient, and very much to Freddie's surprise, Copperhead instructed him to soak Cottonmouth in a warm bath for twenty minutes, and this was to be followed by forcing mineral oil and milk down Cottonmouth's throat to loosen and expel what Copperhead viewed as love-infected fecal stones. "Damned blockages," he stammered to Freddie. "Those nasty hard love fecoliths have to be softened before they can be properly excreted."

"That's the damned love disease for you!" Freddie chimed in.

Ever jubilant over his success rates of treating the most cold-blooded in the reptilian hierarchy, Copperhead giddily began boasting how he had once corrected a dysfunctional bowel movement in old Minnie, a gator in his care. Despondent after her partner's death, she had lapsed into a severe state of dementia, gasping and calling out for her mate one final time before she expired.

"Yes," said Copperhead dolefully, "I am not ashamed to admit that I still wear a black band tied around my heart for my sweet Minnie."

Having unloaded his sorrow, Copperhead informed Freddie that Cottonmouth would have to void an unimaginable amount of love feces, but after a time he would make a complete recovery.

"A lot of AEMI making the rounds in these parts – with its resultant fever, diarrhea and vomiting. His poop is a little off-colour, it's yellow and not quite the soft black or brown stools we expect from a love-free healthy male. I have given him an ultra-sound; his vital organs all seem fine. Now, make sure your hands don't come in contact with any of his feces."

"They won't," Freddie blurted, his voice quivering in terror.

The Silent Treatment

Cottonmouth was fed up with Freddie. He resented being probed by Dr. Copperhead, felt violated and ashamed, but what further shivered his rattle was the double ritual he endured, starting with the morning milking of his venom, followed by a vigorous expulsion of what Freddie came to view as Cottonmouth's appalling "love stools." He had to treat Cottonmouth the way a parent would encourage an irate child to take his medicine.

With a comforting expression on his face, Freddie tasted the mineral oil and milk combo on a soup spoon. "Yummy, so delicious," he declared, licking his lips. Cottonmouth shook his head menacingly at Freddie.

"It's for your own good," said Freddie, at which Cottonmouth emitted a loud contemptuous hiss, while attempting to lunge and deep-fang Freddie's elbow-length rubber gauntlet-styled gloves, the type that sanitation workers use when handling hazardous waste material like corroding metal containers filled with oozing radioactive sludge.

Freddie usually handled Cottonmouth with his bare hands when it came to milking his pal's "gummies," but this time, heeding Copperhead's warning of the highly infectious nature of AEMI, he decided to go gloved, at least until the last of those love stools were voided.

It was only a matter of a few weeks, he thought, before Cottonmouth would be disease-free and could once again share his pillow, but until then, he would have to sleep in the bathtub; which was a problem since Freddie rarely bathed, and wasn't at all inclined to bathe an aquaphobe like Cottonmouth. Still, yet his heart gladdened in recalling a playful Snarlowe flopping noisily around in the tub, taking generous swallows of the bathtub water. Good old Snarlowe of blessed memory. Sure, the case could be made he was a thieving canine, yet that mutt was so affectionate, not at all like Cottonmouth who was now giving him the silent treatment.

As a precautionary step in preventing the spread of AEMI to Freddie's bed and pillow, Cottonmouth was confined to the bathroom at bedtime. Yet in the morning, when he was temporarily freed from the confines of the bathroom, forced to swallow the humiliating stool softening elixir, he detected Hilda's viperous scent and longed for the day he could finally have his beloved all to his own.

He made one last attempt to bite through Freddie's gloves, but it was futile, and to add to his frustration, Freddie made sure that every drop of Copperhead's purgative was swallowed by Cottonmouth.

"Down the hatch, little buddy," cooed Freddie. "Now that wasn't so bad was it?" Cottonmouth shook his head in protest while directing the very tip of his tail at Freddie and daring him to smooch it.

His Affectionate Lasso

For a whole month Cottonmouth was confined to Freddie's bathroom in the evenings. It was quarantine hell for him. With his head pressed against the bathroom door he would listen to his rival making whoopee with Hilda, mounting her and bucking wildly like he was doing the swamp boogie. She viewed Cottonmouth's absence in their frolicking with suspicion, and Freddie's stubborn refusal to free Cottonmouth from the bathroom upset her.

"But why?" she pleaded. Freddie patiently began explaining the circumstances that had lead up to Cottonmouth being sent into isolation. Hadn't he taken into account Cottonmouth's obsessiveness on the matter of cleanliness? With that in mind, Freddie had done his best to bear down and scrub with bleach until the ugly patina left over from his distillery days was no longer evident, and Cottonmouth deemed it clean enough to catch some shut-eye inside the tub.

Again, Hilda entreated Freddie to free Cottonmouth.

"My sweetie is suffering. Can't you hear him crying? He's hurting," she demurred. "Let him go free!"

"Damn it," roared Freddie, "he tore Bruce to pieces and mauled my other ties. They can't wiggle and hiss like they used to. I tell you he's not in his right head. I can't take the chance in freeing him and then have him attack you."

"Have you fed him recently," murmured Hilda silkily. "He must be famished. You're taking out far more than you're putting in. Soon he won't have the juice to squeeze me and I need my squeezies. Let my sweetie out."

At first Freddie was puzzled by Hilda's concern over Cottonmouth's well-being, but then it dawned on him: his companion had recently refused to chow down on a squiggly newborn marsh rice rat. Freddie wondered if Cottonmouth was on some hunger strike to protest his bathroom incarceration, and Freddie's own role as caregiver in ridding him of the dreaded AEMI.

Realizing that Cottonmouth could waste away from his hunger and die, Freddie allowed him to slither out of the bathroom where he soon sidled up to Hilda, lassoing one of her legs with passionate pressure before releasing his affectionate grip.

Viewing their lovey-dovey reunion, something inside Freddie snapped and he bellowed, "Do I get a lick of thanks for helping you get rid of your love stools?"

Grinning, Cottonmouth instantly turned the tip of his tail toward Freddie, and to further provoke him, he hissed long and scornfully, followed by what sounded to Freddie like garburated cuss words. In the silence that followed, a smile appeared to form on Cottonmouth's face.

Freddie was convinced that a malignant force was behind that grin. Turning to Hilda for solace, he blurted out his frustration in having to deal with Cottonmouth's mood disorder.

"He's been giving me the silent treatment, not that he ever had anything important to say to me. There was a time he'd let me crash into his dreams. Now he's all locked up tight like a gated community. And it gets worse. Gabe won't answer my messages because my little buddy, when he could talk, made some obscene pillow calls to him. You see, Gabe is wired to some kind of crazy call display. "

Freddie's face suddenly flushed red. It didn't seem manly for him to fess up and reveal all his vulnerabilities to a free-range swamp hottie. Hilda cast a sideways glance at Cottonmouth, who daintily hissed to signal it was time for another round of lasso foreplay to culminate in the longed-for "squeezies."

Yessie told Freddie he believed his mother could read his thoughts. She was horrified that her boy nurtured wicked carnal reveries about some swamp floozy, and to make his life even more stressful, recurrent bouts of tinnitus plagued him. He swore it sounded like a freight train whistling through an endless tunnel.

"Frrrrrrrrrrrrrruck, mother is killing me – always giving me shit. Why won't she leave me alone? I have always been a good son to her."

Freddie sensed the urgency of the situation. Yessie was heading for the cashew farm to join all the other nutters. Something had to be done and soon. That vision seedling had to be, as they say in the mob, whacked!

"Frrrrrrrrrrrrrruck," stammered Yessie with a twitch in his right eye. "Hey, man, I'm not moving in on your woman. It's just that mother doesn't much care for loose women. She thinks I'm sweet on Hilda."

Yessie's twitch had now moved to his left eye.

"No need to explain" interrupted Freddie. "I understand the living hell she's putting you through. I really do."

"You mustn't say hell," jabbered Yessie. "Momma doesn't like that word."

Freddie sensed that the tectonic plates in Yessie's psyche were already shifting and jostling like denizens of a metal club and the quake to come would engulf what little was left of Yessie's sanity with a tsunami of madness. Yes, that wee pestilential eye had to be whacked to free Yessie of his mother's subjugation.

Yessie would be invited to Freddie's place to try some moonshine which Freddie had purchased from Doctor Melon, who ran an illicit distillery with the help of his assistant Laura. Together they concocted mortuary hooch, so potent that Melon claimed it could stimulate frizzy hair on a bald corpse. He was in mind to market the product as a hair restorer.

Once Yessie was properly blottoed, Freddie would use a tiny mother-of-pearl spoon given to him by his late granny to scoop out Yessie's furtive peeper. It was the perfect surgical instrument and he owed it all to Grandma Betty. She had used that very spoon to convey a measured dollop of black Russian caviar, chilled on a silver tray of chipped ice, over to an unsalted biscuit she firmly held in a lacy gloved hand.

The gourmet purist in Betty had once feared that her expensive caviar would become contaminated if it ever came in contact with her naked hand, and now the heirloom she left Freddie would be put to murderous use by an un-gloved hand. The sacrilege was enough to send Betty's ghost into a twist in her sealed crypt.

"By the way," said Yessie smirking, "your lady was seen riding on the back of Handsome Harry. I thought you ought to know that whore is two-timing you." Freddie was startled by the news. "Not him," gasped Freddie. "He's not her type. She's just using him for a joy ride. Why, that big crazy gator has even given my little buddy a ride."

Yessie grinned an even larger smirk and shook his head. Freddie just wasn't getting it. "That whore is making it with Handsome Harry."

Yessie waited a few seconds to let the news sink into the ear canals of Freddie's wax-packed ears, and then he roared: "What's the matter with you? Are you deaf? I tell you she's going horizontal with him!"

"I don't believe it" whimpered Freddie, "She'd be crushed under his weight. That big fellow must weight a few tons."

"Well," guffawed Yessie, "then your whore is straddling him!"

Suddenly Yessie's third eye began blinking erratically. Lucy was listening in on their conversation. Freddie quickly averted his gaze from Yessie's forehead.

"You got that crazy look again. Why are you staring at me like that? Sometimes I think you got x-ray vision and can read my thoughts."

"I don't have that kind of power," Freddie timidly replied, "but your mother does." And it was true: Lucy could read Yessie's sticky thoughts, his desperate desire to mount Hilda, if only to illustrate to her that lying down with multiple fornicators would put her in a class of a latter day Whore of Babylon and bring ruin upon her. Yessie could never accept the pagan vision of Hilda riding on the back of a lustful gator of gargantuan proportions. He envisioned Hilda instead as a "whore of whores," a devil woman riding a seven-headed beast with ten horns trotting straight out of

Revelation 17:16. That beast would flame her to a crisp and eat her sinful flesh.

Devoid of horns and challenged as far as a head count was concerned, Handsome Harry, despite his devilishly long jaw line endowed with pointy serrated teeth, didn't quite make the fit in New Testament monsterology, a beast the devout could imagine sauntering around the boundless shoreline of the Lake of Fire, nibbling on stubbles of fire and brimstone. That leviathan of Genesis, who swam in a primeval sea, seemed a far more benign creature than the latter, whose handler surely was the devil.

"Hilda, why she is nothing but a no-good whore," continued Yessie, enjoying how it unsettled Freddie to learn of Hilda's infidelity with an alpha gator who the locals called Handsome Harry or, at times, HH. It soon became obvious to Freddie that his friend had become hopelessly addicted to the whore word, unable even to use such synonyms as hussy or trollop instead.

His mother had evoked the syllable often enough when ranting against the practices of fornication relating to adultery and ruttish sex outside of marriage causing an affront to God's Ten Commandments. She gustily equated both transgressions with the frenzied behaviour of barnyard animals. Fornication became one of many hand-me-down words she passed on to Yessie.

Yessie noticed that in all of Lucy's tirades against fornication, certain creatures like honeybees and hummingbirds were exempt from the charge. In her eyes, they were unblemished gifts given to the righteous by the Maker.

As Lucy ranted, her breathing became laboured, but finally, after a few wheezes and gasps, she managed to blurt out, "I hear your father and his whore screaming. The wrathful flames are consuming them. Hallelujah!"

She would then clap her frail hands and point a sclerotic finger at Yessie before letting out a vitriolic torrent against "the legions of fornicators and whores." So passionate was her declaration that it shook a wattle of yellowing skin under her chin.

"They'll sizzle well in the Lake of Fire," she cackled, "and hell you'll go to if you don't mend your ways." Now a smile would curve on her pale lips while her tongue flew back into her toothless mouth.

Yessie was mesmerized by her pinkish tongue, the tip of which was split into two like the forked tongue of a viper, and when she scolded him her tongue vibrated. A bewildered Yessie sensed that it was sniffing out a lingering obscenity which had gone astray like a feral cat. He had to be on his guard to have no other woman enter his mind but his mother. She had protectively bedded down with him from the time he was a babe until he was well into his late teens.

It was only when gossip made the rounds among the pious congregants at her church that the two were indulging in some kind of aberrant behaviour that her pastor requested that she boot him out of her bed and house. Shortly after that he developed what he would later designate as his "twitchies," and to complicate his life further, an involuntary swearing disorder followed. Often times, when he was emotionally overwrought, the two worked in sync to plague him.

"Mind my warning. You're facing double time, a Second Death!" She took a moment to draw in her viper-like tongue, wiped some drool off her pallid lips, and, with a hiss of delight, proceeded to get her chilling message across to him.

"The first time you'll be feeding those earth worms because worms have to eat – and then you'll end up frying in that blazing lake. The goated one will have his foul way with you."

Long after Lucy shuffled off her mortal coil, he dwelt on those terrifying moments when his raging mother worked herself into sweat, vocalizing on Revelation 20: 14-15. There was cold comfort in knowing he wouldn't be frying alone in that fiery lake:

Freddie and Hilda would join him there, so would his dad, his dad's whore and other countless fornicators, so many his mother declaimed, that had they all queued up in single file, they would have formed a chain of sinners far exceeding the length of the Earth's diameter.

She Was His Butterfly

Freddie often wondered how a gator who was anything but handsome had come to earn the unusual sobriquet Handsome Harry. He was amazed to learn that the name had something to do with the sudden disappearance of a good-looking tall blond dude by the name of Harry Longshanks. A natural born lady-killer, he was much sought after by rich housewives in Gorgonia. They were only too glad to provide for his creature comforts either in cash, or have him attired in James Bond-styled two-button conduit-cut suits with tailored shirts and matching silk ties, all of which served to accentuate his physical prowess as a top-of-the-line stud.

Added to this, he made clever use of very expensive designer pheromone cologne, which when combined with his own natural pheromone, made him doubly attractive to his bevy of women. However, a luxuriant lifestyle can end up as roadkill. There is a price tag that comes with being a reckless boy toy having dalliances with the wives of rich and powerful men who would think nothing of doing away with him. It was a short time after one of his amorous indiscretions that he disappeared. It was said, by a few of his friends, that he left Gorgonia and set up his practice elsewhere after being warned that a contract had been put out to whack him. A few Gorgonian insiders claimed to the contrary that Longshanks met a violent end at the hands of a professional hitman hired by some vengeful husband, who, according to some gossipers, had paid an additional bonus to have Longshanks' manhood severed, luxuriously gift-wrapped and parcel-posted to the cheating wife.

Other rumours abounded, but one concerning Longshanks' disappearance was particularly redolent with gruesome savagery: being the amateur lepidopterist, a hooped twelve-inch diameter butterfly net in hand, the story was that he had he set out to hunt for the evasive Giant Swallowtail and somewhere en route to capture this extraordinary butterfly, he met up with an enormous gator who was waiting behind some palm fronds to ambush him.

In seconds the beast had clamped his jaws firmly on Longshanks' legs, and soon there was nothing left of him but a runny pulp protein soaked in blood and a heap of fragmented bones.

Such was the terror of this awesome killing machine that a few members in the gator-hunting fraternity, after a boozy gabfest, decided to bestow an honorific on Longshanks' killer. They named him Handsome Harry and it stuck as a twisted memorial to his victim, even if, at the time, there wasn't a *corpus delicti* to prove that the humungous gator had actually devoured poor Harry Longshanks, that is, unless one was prepared to believe a town drunk by the name of Tommy Witherspoon who, according to some of his imbibing sidekicks, would have sold one of his kidneys for a drink.

He maintained that he had witnessed the actual ambush yet suggested Longshanks was seen dallying with Hilda shortly before he met his untimely fate.

The weekend evening crowd at the Pink Cygnet Pub, located in a seedier section of Gorgonia, desperately wanted to believe Witherspoon. They were especially titillated each time he made Longshanks' violent end more macabre.

"You know, guys, I still hear his bones crackling in my dreams like they were matchsticks and his blood is a-gushing. Hey, fellows, I could use another drink." A beardy listener closest to the bar signalled the bartender and, in a jiff, Witherspoon's glass was topped with the cheapest bourbon in the house, and soon a freshened account of Longshanks' gristly death followed.

"I tell you that gator was the biggest damned bastard I'd ever seen."

"What do you reckon his size was?" someone asked. Witherspoon at first hesitated and then, scratching his forehead as though to stimulate memory, cautiously replied, "Maybe twenty feet? Now I could be mistaken – I say that gator was closer to thirty feet, maybe forty?"

Looking around him at the dazed expression of his enraptured audience, Witherspoon decided on the spot to offer some compelling evidence to substantiate his story about his Longshanks sighting and the toothy berserker who did him in.

"Yep, fellows, I got something you all want to see that belonged to the kid."

"Hey, like maybe his cojones," someone chortled, a guffaw which proved contagious as soon everyone started cachinnating. It upset Witherspoon, but he managed to maintain his comportment and demanded another drink, if only to compensate him for his injured dignity, and once again his glass was refreshed.

"What you got, Witherspoon?" someone yelled. Others joined in, demanding to see what Witherspoon had in his possession that had once belonged to Longshanks.

"I found this beaut of a case not far from where that gator tore up that boy." And with that, Witherspoon laid an oval-shaped large gold compact encrusted with tiny lapis lazuli gems on the bar. To indicate who the previous owner was, the compact was clearly engraved in pure white silver with the initials HL.

A flurry of faces crowded around the compact as Witherspoon slowly opened it to pull out an unused condom in mint condition; its soft-jellied surface was embossed with blistery nodules intended to provide maximum stimulation for any of Longshanks' women craving the ultimate in sexual satisfaction.

"It's a French tickler," Witherspoon proudly announced, holding it up for all to see, "and if you want to touch it, it'll cost you another drink." Witherspoon downed his drink and chuckled.

"At least he had his fun with that devil woman. I guess she was his butterfly."

Fresh Meat

Fearing they would end up as luncheon meat, most home boys never set out to nab Handsome Harry, not if their screws weren't loose. Handsome Harry continued to instill a piss-inducing fear in the lot, and it earned him a triumphal respect, especially by the Gorgonian soldiers of the Azazel crime family. That gang covered up their criminal activities in Gorgonia by claiming they were decent hard-working businessmen running a legitimate waste management disposal business, and going so far as to claim that their firm, Cygnus Sanitation Services, was truly an environmentally friendly operation.

The truth was, however, that the company was anything but mindful of the environment. Nah, the bastards dumped hazardous industrial materials in pristine waterways teeming with trout. They had one particular dumping ground in mind this time, but it wasn't to unload PCBs, cadmium and mercury-filled containers. Still, it was a societal element just as toxic, as they disposed of the corpses of troublesome thugs decommissioned in one whack job after another, usually done with a 22-calibre handgun equipped with a silencer, two shots to the head. Foof! Foof!

Those flashy suited wise guys frequently made use of a pathway fringing the swamp that they called Harry's Alley after observing that legendary gator roaming leisurely about as though he didn't give a fig for diddly. For those gunsels, it seemed the perfect place to ditch a fresh kill and see it quickly macerated before their eyes. Handsome Harry couldn't believe his luck, and it soon dawned on him that he had formed a copacetic relationship with the mob. All that was required of him was to devour each cadaver with gratitude, slapping his tail and then emitting a loud hiss of jubilation or, at times, breaking wind just as his benefactors were about to leave him to his feeding.

On one such occasion chowing down, a bonhumous mobster called Frank the Ice Man by his respectful associates (his specialty: inserting an ice pick into a targeted ear in what he called "a wax job") whipped around and taunted Handsome Harry. "Hey, greedy guts," Frank chuckled. "Dummy, there's more meat coming your way today so leave some room for the next delivery."

So often did the gang arrive with their meaty deposits that it instilled a feeling of satiated well-being in Handsome Harry. But what was he to do with his abundant provisions? Was he to share them with his own kind? There was no way he would divvy up his fast food with any of his gladiatorial cohorts.

He suffered from an inborn greed that began the instant he popped out of the eggshell. His was a classic example of a dysfunctional family. Being the least favourite in the brood, he was the last to be fed by his mother. As a result, his food portions were smaller than his brothers' and sisters', and it wasn't long before he started treating each meal as though it were his last, and so with it began an almost idolatrous worship of food. Handsome Harry developed a food-hoarding condition which he couldn't shake off as he approached adulthood. He always felt famished, even when his guts bulged with the tastiest vittles.

As the cadavers piled up, his providers were treated to a strange ritual. They witnessed Handsome Harry dragging a corpse down the sludgy banks and submerging it in the acidic swampy water for hours. It was as though he knew instinctively that he had his own way of marinating the meat, thus tenderizing it and making it more favorable to his taste buds. In addition, the marinating process preserved what remained of the meat so when he was inclined, he could come back to snack on some leftovers.

But sometimes the chow came with an unexpected condiment. He found himself chomping on the odd Rolex watch which hadn't been liberated by a shooter. Chewing down on that expensive time piece gave him painful intestinal gas, yet he was not averse to mawing down on a corpse dressed in an Armani suit; he found the silken fabric curiously tasty.

However, he took a deep offence to any corpse wearing top-of-the line handcrafted gator skin footwear. Gnashing his teeth, he was both grieved and horrified at that patterned gator skin which might have once belonged to a loved one. Handsome Harry's chagrin didn't go unnoticed. It stirred compassion in the godfather Tony Azazel. Towering close to seven feet in his special elevated shoes, he instructed his underlings to "show some respect" for the bereaved gator. There was a noticeable soft spot in Tony, especially when it came to widows, orphans and uncontrollably weeping gators. Tears leaked from the corners of his grey eyes as a telltale sign of empathy.

But he shied away from revealing his more sensitive side, fearing others would take him for a sissy and then he would have to resort to unspeakable acts of violence to prove his inherent masculinity. Fear brought about respect and Tony loved that word. He wanted foe and friend alike to stare mawkishly up at him as though he were some god to be revered; worshipping any other deity but him was a dastardly betrayal.

Tony's soldiers first gawped at his heightened shoes and then up to his scarred moon-shaped face with its full Van Dyke goatee, which quivered when he barked out his orders. His subordinates knew better than to quibble with their boss, who as a child had a rubber baby gator he splashed around with in the tub. Those childhood memories were deeply embedded in his soul and so he wasn't going to stand for any of his boys harming a gator let alone ridiculing a creature such as Handsome Harry.

The wise guys were ordered to remove any gator-leathered footwear of gang members they were assigned to kill; Handsome Harry could now sidle up, inhale an offering, and detecting no gator odour, enjoy sinking his teeth down on a foot without having to gawk at an abomination of a buffed Ferrini alligator shoe.

Housefly

When Yessie babbled that some morbidly obese housefly on his kitchen table was talking to him, Freddie realized he could no longer delay Operation Pipsqueak, his murderous plan to scoop out Yessie's pestilential third eye, using what he determined to be the perfect surgical tool – his tiny mother-of-pearl caviar spoon. He had locked away that family heirloom in a drawer along with a three-dollar Mickey Mouse wristwatch his granny had purchased in 1933. Yet what sent a frisson of fear deep into his guts was the thought that he could only rely on himself to carry out this whack job.

There was a time when Freddie could count on Bruce's sage advice in dealing with life's predicaments, such as the unpleasant task he would soon have to undertake to save Yessie's sanity, but that alpha snake tie was now shredded, a victim of one of Cottonmouth's hissy fits. Freddie had reverently placed Bruce's remains in an indigo blue velvet tie purse that his aunt Minnie purchased in Thailand, where she had traipsed about seeking Buddhist enlightenment as a faux hippy among the temples and ruins of Wat Mahathat. Minnie's purse could absorb a surprising amount of tears.

However, there were moments when Freddie thought the contents entombed in the purse had transmuted into a weeping ghost. Freddie reasoned that the tears didn't belong to him but to spooky Bruce.

Often Freddie would inhale Bruce's tears which saturated that unique funereal purse and detect a sweet frangipani fragrance that awed and terrified him. He would then quickly put the purse away in a corner of his clothes closet while his other snaky ties stirred and ululated. They missed the materiality that once belonged to the living Bruce, an alpha male snake tie among male snaky neckwear. Denied the pleasure of his corporeal company, they now found solace in communicating with his spirit.

Freddie cast a despairing eye on Cottonmouth. For a brief moment he imagined that his little buddy would emit a few sibilated sounds indicating his support for Operation Pipsqueak. But none came. Cottonmouth, instead, stared icily at him and yawned. There was something disparaging in that yawn, a gape which kept widening in its derision of Freddie, its malice further engorged by a split tongue vibrating like a bendable tuning fork.

Cottonmouth's uncoiling tongue chilled Gabriel. He was convinced that Cottonmouth was the devil. Cottonmouth's vibratory appendage matched up to the very reptile who conned Eve into taking a bite out of an apple from the verboten Tree of Knowledge in the Garden of Eden, resulting in an eviction notice from the Maker for Eve and her beau.

Realizing the potential mischief that Cottonmouth's deceitful tongue could cause, Freddie wondered if he could count on Cottonmouth to speak to no one, especially not to Yessie after his rogue eye had been removed along with its embedded Lucy.

Although they still shared the same pillow, his little buddy had stopped conversing with him. Not only had Cottonmouth gone silent on Freddie, he had gated the entry to his dreams and there was no special back entrance such as one would find at a Tudor manor for tradesmen. Any act of violence went against Freddie's nature. He needed the courage that came in a bottle of Dr. Melon's "Fire Bull Surprise" (not to be confused with another surprise in the shape of a metal bull called "Brazen Bull" heated up to cook its victims alive) to anaesthetize Yessie and carry through with the surgery.

Yessie's eyelids began to twitch, and soon his whole face appeared to quiver as though at that moment the tectonic plates of what remained of his sanity were being squeezed together.

"I'm telling you Mother's voice was coming from that fffffffffffffrucken fly."

Green as Green Could Be

When Laura née Dewberry wasn't touching up an unsightly disfigurement on the face of a cadaver at Melon's mortuary, she was busily working at colourizing illicit booze. In a magical instant she could make a garishly coloured moonshine more appealing to the eyes of hard-drinking consumers, who would have blanched at the sight of a forest-green concoction that might have escaped from the butthole of an irritable bowel sufferer. Laura was astonished to find that her off and on again boyfriend, the very brute who assassinated Hilda's lover, Porco Pete, liked his hooch "in the raw," untreated by Laura's aesthetic colouring. He bristled utterly to Laura's choice of what he viewed as "kissy colours," and of those "girly" hues, it was pink which rankled him the most.

He claimed that a lengthy exposure to the most effeminate of colours would shrink the cojones on a real man down to the size of a grape seed. Laura's man, a meat-and-potatoes sort of guy, was a thirties and forties cinephile who never warmed up to the idea of colourizing oldie cartoon creatures like those animated black and white Merrie Melodies characters – Porky Pig in a duck hunter's drag aiming a double-barrelled shotgun at a babbling Daffy Duck, or threatening to blow away a psychotic "wabbit" like Bugs Bunny, nervously nibbling a long tapered carrot while trying to talk his stuttering adversary out of shooting him.

The controller would have none of Laura "tarting up" the pure product, sedimented as it was, and green as green could be. But what he fancied most was a suppliant Laura who would give into his every whim. Drool slid down his frazzled beard as he tried to calm an irrepressible urge to undress Laura, strap her down in the buff on a hydraulic mortuary operating table and bathe her in a green giggle juice of his own choosing, starting from her chin down to her Venus mound and onto silver lacquered toenails and, to add more fuel to drive his amatory mojo,

Laura had shown him the dildo which Freddie had given her in lieu of cash for a magnum bottle of her finest distilled liquor. It was during this transaction that she promised Freddie that she would never again involve an innocent like Cottonmouth whenever she chose to work the graveyard shift birching Dr. Melon's buns to the strains of a cassette-taped ode to Brünnhilde's Immolation in Wagner's opera *Gotterdammerung*.

Laura stared into her boyfriend's beastly eyes. Suddenly her mind conjoined with his, and it frightened her to think that her lissome body would be laved in an impure concoction that she generally sold to ruffian guzzlers (she wouldn't have stooped to wash her feet with that vulgar effluent) rather than Fire Bull Surprise, which she insisted had ethereal properties that charged out like a bull in heat to captivate the senses of the discriminating imbiber.

That Babbling Corpse

Although Freddie never revealed the core reason for his purchase to Laura, he was assured by her that Fire Bull Surprise wouldn't disappoint the imbiber. Needing the extra cash she earned from the illicit sales of that libation, Laura wasn't one to ask whether some thirsty consumer would make ill-use of the product, but as Freddie was to find out, she had a few surprises of her own which didn't come in a bottle.

She told him that late one evening, while working on a corpse with the due diligence that was expected of her as a dedicated mortuary artist, she desperately needed an upper tonic to recharge her batteries, so she took a miniscule swig of Fire Bull Surprise and, in doing so, accidentally spilled a few droplets on her subject's mouth. To her horror, the dead man's lips quivered, and in the seconds that followed, his tongue flew out of his mouth to lick that elixir. But what proved even more spectacular to Laura, the cadaver's eyelids suddenly opened.

Staring up at Laura, a pair of grey blue eyes emitted a luminescence that one might expect from a lantern fish haunting some tropical coral reef. Laura confided to Freddie that the words issuing from the mouth of that babbling corpse still haunted her. So traumatized was she by that horrific experience, she was on the cusp of asking for a week's sick leave. Again and again she heard the deceased plead "Ummmmmmmmmmm, so good, more, please – I want more..."

"So then what happened?" Freddie asked breathlessly, unable to contain his excitement. If a few drops of Fire Bull Surprise could bring momentary life to a stiff, then surely a more generous swallow of that miraculous potation, he reasoned, could revitalize Yessie and prevent Lucy's malevolent spirit from further haunting his head and nibbling away at what remained of her son's grey matter.

"I'll have you know," chirped Laura, "that my Fire Bull Surprise was much appreciated by Mutt Lafarge, you know, he's that poor man who got done in by Porco Pete."

"I don't believe it," Freddie exclaimed. "You mean to tell me you fed him some of your grog? Now, was it before or was it after his head got placed in Melon's fancy sphere for a snazzy burial?"

Laura discerned a condescending smile forming on Freddie's mouth. He tried to muffle the laugh that followed and only succeeded in partially muzzling it. (For just an instant Laura delighted in the thought that she would one day have the opportunity to apply her painterly skills on Freddie and, in the process, let a tiny bit of her magic potion slip down his throat. The thought of Freddie begging her for more Fire Bull Surprise aroused a delightful quiver in her that induced her to leak a treacly smile.) It didn't take Laura long to realize that Freddie was joshing her, yet she kept her cool.

"It was just shortly after I combed his hair," she continued. "Why, I thought that he deserved a drink after what he went through. Imagine getting ripped apart by that mean Porco Pete. And so I opened Mutt's mouth and poured in a smidgen of Fire Bull Surprise, and would you believe, he opened his eyes, and thanked me, said it beat the best Bourbon he ever tasted by a country mile, and then, amazingly, that kind man closed his eyes, smiled and died." Freddie soon began to tire of Laura's stories about her reanimating the dead. It made him feel nauseous. He told her he had to hurry back home fearing, that Cottonmouth would be suffering his usual bout of separation anxiety if he didn't promptly return.

"You're not going to give him Fire Bull Surprise are you?" said Laura with a tremor of apprehension in her voice for Cottonmouth's well-being.

Freddie looked menacingly at her, and by his stare she realized that Cottonmouth had spilled the beans. Freddie already knew how Cottonmouth was forced to fetch the very whip which Laura used to turn Melon's butt into a topographic map of raised welts and patches of blood.

"My little buddy won't be playing fetch with you ever again," he shouted, and with that he picked up his tall bottle of Firebull Surprise, stashed it in a brown paper bag, and left.

Quintessential Snake

Freddie decided to test out the potency of Fire Bull Surprise on Cottonmouth. He would sprinkle a few drops on the head of a live rodent he intended to serve up as a meal for his little buddy. The experiment would take place shortly after the usual morning extraction of Cottonmouth's venom when he would be famished, as was the case after every morning milking session. Swept up in the intensity of swallowing Freddie's offering head first, it would never occur to Cottonmouth that his wriggly chow being turned into liquid protein had been anointed with a few droplets of Laura's miraculous libation. For Cottonmouth, ingesting that rat seemed every bit as pleasurable as applying his squeezies on Hilda. In her own right, she was a meal which nourished his love for the quintessential snake in her.

Freddie began to imagine that there were other benefits to the Surprise besides turning off the lights in Yessie's noggin. He fancied there were some active ingredients in the Surprise which would enable him to pacify Cottonmouth, quell the testiness in him, making that viper more tolerable to live with.

Gazing down on Cottonmouth's lidless eyes, Freddie noted that they glistened with a sparkly contentment. But more astonishing, an intractable smile had formed on Cottonmouth's lips, conveying an impression that his tongue was forever locked inside his mouth, while at the same moment he lapsed into a deep sleep, so that no matter how hard Freddie shook him, he couldn't be awakened.

The only telltale sign indicating that Cottonmouth was still alive was a rippling sound in his belly, which Freddie perceived to be stomach acid slowly eating away what remained of that rodent forming a bulge inside Cottonmouth's innards. Freddie, although he was a tad revolted by that vulgar digestive workout, was nevertheless elated, for the Surprise was just what he needed to send Yessie adrift on a dream cloud, while he readied his granny's caviar spoon to evict that pesky vision seed along with its embedded evil tenant.

It was a good several hours before Cottonmouth awoke. He immediately began to suspect there was something amiss, as he had never fallen asleep while devouring a toothsome meal which gratified his taste buds. Feeling that his gastric dignity had somehow been violated, he searched Freddie's eyes in a gaze so powerful it bent Freddie's will, forcing him to come clean and admit his guilt and the reason for conducting a shameless experiment on his little buddy.

"You asphole, how dare you do this to me!" he cried. The invective was followed by a loud sibilance which jetted out of his mouth. Freddie was taken aback. Cottonmouth had found his voice again, and Freddie dimly realized that this voice sizzled with an irrepressible rage.

It was bad enough for Cottonmouth having to put up with Dr. Copperhead's medication designed to excrete those love bugs, his being incarcerated in Freddie's bathroom which served as isolation ward for the highly infectious AEMI – and if this wasn't punishing enough, being further aggrieved in picking up seismic noises of Freddie and Hilda making out lasciviously in the bedroom – but now he had been used in lieu of a lab rat as an experimental subject to test the effectiveness of Fire Bull Surprise. It was more than he could bear. No self-respecting reptile would put up with that "bull ssssssssheet!"

Freddie looked pleadingly at Cottonmouth, hoping that his anger would somehow subside so he could talk some sense into him. But Cottonmouth was having none of it. Having declaimed his furies, he slithered away and as he did, he curled up the very tip of his tail, aiming it at Freddie.

"Kiss it, pal, give it a ssssssssssssssssssssmooooooch."

In a Digestive Sense

The third eye had to be whacked and soon. Freddie realized he would get no support from Cottonmouth in eliminating Yessie's third eye. He tried to incite Cottonmouth against Yessie by informing him that he had once offered to purchase him for the purpose of rendering his skin into high-end exotic leatherwear. This revelation seemed to have no effect on Cottonmouth, who made no attempt to suppress a yawn.

"You owe me, little buddy," said Freddie, irritated by Cottonmouth's behaviour. "Look here, if I didn't turn down Yessie's offer to buy you – and he offered me plenty of money – why, you'd have ended up being a fancy leather belt."

Freddie began to smirk, and then on impulse and purely for his own amusement added, "There just might have been just enough of your skin left over to make some buffed leather for a pair of fancy cowboy boots for a toddler, or a midget. Now, is it too much to ask for you to be my lookout in case someone decides to come calling the minute I am having the third eye whacked? What do you say, little buddy?"

A stony silence followed. Cottonmouth was apparently holding his vocalizations back for a more opportune time when he could vent his fury to the maximum in one convulsive moment. Freddie thought he would give it one more shot. Surely, he thought, there was a spot of guilt in Cottonmouth. Didn't he realize that Freddie had saved his skin?

"What do you say, little buddy?"

Cottonmouth wasn't saying anything. He made no attempt to acknowledge that he had heard Freddie's request, and no matter how many times Freddie tried to lather guilt on Cottonmouth, and he laid it on thick, blathering over and over again that he was owed a favour, in the end his begging came to naught. It wasn't so much that Cottonmouth was taking pleasure in humiliating Freddie, he simply had no idea what guilt meant. In a digestive sense, guilt meant nothing to him: *guilt was invisible, odourless and, worse, tasteless.*

That Crazy Eye Is Just Another Fish Egg

Life went on as usual in Freddie's neighbourhood. Handsome Harry kept dining on corpses on his turf disposed of by the Azazel crime family in Gorgonia, and big Tony Azazel, ever mindful of cannibalistic features in the food intake sustaining his adoptive eating machine, made doubly sure that none of the besuited dead wore gator skin footwear, or pricey gator skin jeans and jackets. *H.H. was family* as far as Tony was concerned.

Freddie had thought of having one of Tony's soldiers come in on whacking the third eye. Freddie had done one or two small favours for Tony and so he thought that Tony would show his gratitude by assigning some goodfella like Frank the Ice Man to take out the third eye. But after taking into account that Frank's specialty was in his masterly use of an ice pick in cleaning out the ear canals of the doomed, Freddie had second thoughts, shuddering at the idea of the third eye being stabbed and popped out of Yessie's forehead by something as fiendishly brutal as a pointy ice pick.

Opting to make good use of Grandma Betty's caviar spoon, he began imagining that Yessie's forehead had been transformed into a plate of ice, and the third eye resting near a clump of frozen sturgeon roe had miraculously changed into a fish egg, ready to be daintily plucked. It would be a joyous whack job. An enraptured Freddie began chanting:

That crazy eye is just another fish egg. That crazy eye is just another fish egg.

"Yes! Yes! Yes!" he cried out ecstatically.

That crazy eye is just another fish egg. That crazy eye is just another fish egg.

Hey, This Drink Is Talking to Me

Cottonmouth decided to slither away in a huff from Freddie's place and meet up with his pal Handsome Harry. With any luck, Hilda would join him again to go for a ride on that big gator's back. He made good his escape before Yessie turned up for a gabfest with Freddie, an exchange of boisterous gossip of whom amongst the gator hunting boys was carrying on with whose wife, but the two were in for a real surprise, especially Freddie who, to his amazement, found that the colour in Fire Bull Surprise had changed from a sanguine red into a rich bluey-green that one might find on a polished turquoise stone ring. It didn't seem to matter to Yessie what colour Laura's crafted mortuary moonshine was, his thirst seemed to be getting the better of him.

He craved being pleasantly stewed, even if Lucy disapproved of him "partaking the fetid contents of Satan's Cup." But what Lucy found more odious than any satanic drink was a lady distiller like canoodling Laura.

"I tell you she's Satan's whore!" Lucy had blustered, splattering Yessie with flying spittle. "She's a-sleeping with the dead, I tell you. Whores like her always do. Just like fleas feeding on a mangy dog." Sometimes her venom would spill over the top, as the time she told him that it would have been better had he been delivered as a stillborn. "Like a dead baby rat," she cackled triumphantly, "in his mother's filthy nest."

Staring dolefully at his glass of Fire Bull Surprise in chromatic flux, tears flowed down Yessie's cheeks. Freddie could feel a force field of sadness emanating toward him as more tears gushed from Yessie's right eye as it twitched and then his left eye spasmed wildly.

"I feel a fruuuuuuuuuuuuuuuking headache coming on. Mother is displeased. Mother! Mother! Mother is killing me. My head is boiling over. Help me, please help me!"

Yessie began to drool into his drink. It was as though he had suddenly developed a bad case of psychic rabies. Gurgling sounds began to issue from his lips which suddenly became greyer than usual, while at that same moment the little robust colour Yessie had in his cheeks began to etiolate.

"Mother!" he yelped one more time. It seemed at that very moment Yessie's soul had become transformed into a nest filled with stillborn baby rats.

"For ffffffffffffrucks sake, down the hatch, fellow," a panic-stricken Freddie squealed, forcing the drink into Yessie's hands, just as another gurgling sound louder than the first rumbled towards Freddie.

"I feel a fruuuuuuuuuuuuuuuking headache coming on...help... help me."

Yessie stared into his drink, which now began to sparkle and spew like fireworks at a KISS concert in the '70s. Freddie stood back, awed by that magical effervescence. But what happened next not only startled him but jangled his nerves, for suddenly Yessie went ballistic and began shouting at Freddie.

"Hey, this drink is talking to me. Mother is trying to reach me."

"That's a lot of bullshit," replied Freddie. "How can she be in that drink?"

"Well," said Yessie, trying to regain his composure, "maybe that bitch in the mortuary has put a bit of Mother into this drink!"

"Down the hatch," roared Freddie, attempting to downplay Yessie's fear. But Yessie was still apprehensive in downing his drink, heeding his mother's warning that he who imbibed with the devil would end up skinny-dipping in the Lake of Fire. But there are times a man has to chase away those rainy day blues, defy the mother that he has been brought up to cherish and obey, and drain away a devilish brew strong enough to sprout hair on a bald corpse stretched out on a mortuary embalming table.

I Won't Drink My Mother

The Fire Bull Surprise soon morphed into a vibrant turquoise which reminded Yessie of the grace that once existed in Lucy's eyes when he was but a toddler and she a young mother, dutifully attending to his nurturing. And then it had to happen: Yessie's father, a drunk and a wastrel, deserted the family home, taking up with another woman! It shattered Lucy, who then changed from a loving mother who once swaddled her son in oodles of affection to a bossy harridan, relentless in directing her anger at the only man left in her life, young Yessie. Later, Lucy took her revenge and found a replacement for the philandering husband who had abandoned her. She fell hopelessly in love with the only man she felt she could trust – Jesus.

"Drink up, my good man, down the hatch!" Yessie kept staring at his glass, brimming with scintillating turquoise vitality. "Mother is a carp," chirped Yessie. "Look! Look! She's waving at me. Mother! Mother! Mother! I am missing you!"

And it was phantasmically true, at least in Yessie's mind, for not only was she signalling him, Lucy's barbels were vibrating as she searched for ghostly edibles with her sensory filaments that whiskered out from her snout. Or was she searching for the truth of her son's transgressions?

"Have you been on some swamp weed?" Freddie bellowed, drawing closer to Yessie's drink and peering into the glass. Was Yessie approaching meltdown? Perhaps, thought Freddie, it was best to humour Yessie, go along with his mother fish, gain his confidence and slowly talk him out of his delusionary state.

Freddie had recently read a news item where a householder had imagined that a moldy loaf of rye bread in the pantry resembled the face of Christ.

"I see your mother. Yes, by golly, it's true. She's waving her fins," said Freddie, fixing a honeyed smile to suit his plastered-on geniality. "What does Mother say?" exclaimed Yessie. Freddie peered into the glass, and while doing so, he noticed that the turquoise was starting to erupt. It seemed as though the drink itself was becoming impatient with its virgin imbiber, the cowering Yessie.

"What's Mother saying?" cried Yessie, terrified.

"I believe," replied Freddie calmly, "she's asking you to down your drink, if I am reading her lips correctly..."

But before Freddie could utter another word, Yessie interjected, challenging Freddie's proficiency at lip-reading. Unruffled, Freddie again peered into the glass, and as he did so, he noticed that the colouration of Fire Bull Surprise was changing to a hue that a botanist might find on a Floridian emerald rose.

"Yes, I can see it now. She wants you to drink up!"

"You can't fool me," Yessie clamoured, "You're no damned fish lip-reader!"

"Drink up," barked Freddie. "Lucy is thirsty. She's waiting for you in your soul."

"No, Freddie. Damn it! I won't drink my Mother!" roared Yessie.

Blub...Blub...Blub...

The Fire Bull Surprise opted for a rose pink red next, and then on a whim flamed into a deep orange. Freddie surmised that some impure catalytic by-product had taken residence in that drink. He was sure the culprit was Lucy.

Blub...blub...blub...

There was something familiar about those piqued eyes.

"You know, Yessie, you just might be right. Yep, it could be Lucy. Weren't her eyes dark brown, or maybe they were grey...or green?"

"Mother, is that really you?" cried Yessie, viewing his mother's displeasure in those fishy eyes as more voluble bubbles issued from an aggressive mouth.

"Mother, don't be angry with your boy – I love you, Mother."

Blub... blub... blub...

Freddie thought he could read those bubbling lips.

"Okay, possum ass, what does Mother say!" snapped Yessie snarkily, hoping to expose Freddie as a fraud in lip-reading.

"No need to get sore, Yessie, it takes time to read those lips. You see, those lips are formed differently than our lips..."

Freddie decided to try a different tact in convincing Yessie to down his Fire Bull Surprise, which was now turning the colour of polished yellow-gold. Staring deeply into Yessie's twitching eyes, and realizing his friend was hopelessly tethered in obeisance to his mother's wishes, Freddie decided to appeal to that controlling mothering core embedded in Yessie's psyche.

"She's waiting down there in your soul. Can't you see it? There's sunlight coming out of her mouth. She's powerfully thirsty."

"Yes, by Jiminy Cricket," crooned Yessie. "Mother is thirsty. I will take that drink right now."

The Percolating Light

To Yessie's astonishment, each time he summoned his courage (with Freddie's dogged support) to make the Fire Bull Surprise a tipple of choice, it mutated in colour, so that one may have assumed there was a temperamental interior decorator embedded in that miraculous libation who was displeased with each hue. The screwy joy emanating from that drink didn't agree with Cottonmouth, and the last thing that Freddie and Yessie expected to hear was an implosive whisper from Cottonmouth.

"You're all aspholes!"

"Slime of Satan!" howled Yessie.

"Don't pay him any heed, drink up," said Freddie.

"Hey there, you aspholes!" lisped Cottonmouth, who would have to come up with another outrageous expletive, as the two were now wise to his clever reptilian behaviour, even if Freddie found Cottonmouth's cussing annoying as it was distracting Yessie from quaffing his Fire Bull Surprise. Maybe, thought Freddie, there was some substance to Cottonmouth's charge that they were both aspholes.

"Down the hatch, fellow" chirped Freddie, making the frantic gestures of a serious guzzler about to pour a highball down his gullet, but Yessie was stalling. His eyes began to sparkle. He began shaking his head in wonderment, as though the child in him had entered an upscale toy store.

"Look at the sunshine," exclaimed Yessie, his face twitching in a rash of delight. "Oh look at that sunshine, oh so pretty!"

"I can't believe it," responded Freddie. "What the deuce is going on here?"

Slowly it began to dawn on Freddie that the percolating sunlight in the Surprise wasn't the Solar Light of Goodness and Redemption, but all that was evil in Lucy. It was Freddie who detected a whiff of sewage gas in that rising incandescence.

Yessie in Flames

Before Freddie had a chance to warn Yessie that the light rising from his glass of Fire Bull Surprise wasn't the light of goodness but an evil emanation of dark forces, Yessie downed his drink, and as he did, he turned as crimson red as the caricature of a heavy metal devil. Freddie thought he heard a gurgling ffff sound issuing from deep inside Yessie's throat. A purply red effluvium poured out of Yessie's mouth. Freddie's keen snout determined it was sulphur. But what amazed Freddie even more was Yessie's final cry, a shriek so hellish it reverberated in Freddie's ears, penetrating his wax-impacted ear canals.

"Mother, I love you!" Yessie squealed like a thrashing banshee, and in the moments that followed, Freddie imagined he heard his long-departed blind pit bull Snarlowe baying in the background as though in sympathy with Yessie's plight. Freddie had miscalculated the proper dosage of Fire Bull Surprise to anaesthetize Yessie. Staring down at Yessie's corpse on the floor and observing the hideous expression on his friend's face, it dawned on him that Yessie's soul was already taking a scorcher of a bath in the Lake of Fire. But what really startled Freddie and sent a chilling frisson down his spine was something he discerned on Yessie's forehead. It wasn't so much Yessie's twitching eyes which glommed on Freddie, phenomenal enough a sight considering that Yessie was as stiff as clapboard; the third eye had returned! And if that wasn't sufficiently frightful, that vision seed was shaking as though someone inside was boisterous with laughter.

"Asphole," hissed Cottonmouth. "Don't you see she's mocking you!"

This Calls for a Whack Job

While Yessie's corpse lay on the floor, Cottonmouth kept calling Freddie an asphole. He kept repeating that expletive until it began to unnerve Freddie. But what was more unsettling than Cottonmouth's delight in riling Freddie was the reappearance of the third eye. It sent a frisson of terror deep into Freddie's innards. In plain sight, that vision seed was blinking its defiance at Freddie. Cottonmouth continued baiting him, but his gums were hurting. Freddie had applied more than the usual pressure in his morning ritual in squeezing out every drop of Cottonmouth's venom.

"Back off, little buddy," yowled Freddie.

Glaring contemptuously at Freddie, Cottonmouth released a loud hiss, but found he couldn't articulate the one phrase he had become enamoured with. He suddenly found himself voiceless, unable to utter "asphole."

"Say," said Freddie mockingly, "are you trying to say something, little buddy?"

But Cottonmouth now found another way of expressing himself. His split tongue flew out of his mouth, vibrating in the direction of the third eye. It was blinking defiantly at Freddie. The third eye was not only rocking with Lucy's triumphal cackling, but rattling Freddie as well. Freddie's predicament gave much pleasure to Cottonmouth. And while it was true he hated Lucy, and would have deeply fanged her if ever the opportunity presented itself, seeing the look of fear in Freddie's eyes made it all seem worthwhile for Cottonmouth.

"Damn! Damn! Damn!" cried Freddie, spooked by the reemergence of the third eye.

"This calls for a whack job." He would now put his granny's mother-of-pearl spoon to good use in extracting that dreaded vision seed and its enclosed wraith, the tenant Lucy. They would both be promptly evicted from Yessie's stone cold forehead.

Yessie's Final Liberating Cry

The time had arrived for Freddie to put Grandma Betty's treasured heirloom to sweet morbid use. With it in hand, he leaned over Yessie's frozen forehead to locate a barely perceptible third eye, and soon he locked on to an object no bigger than a pin prick.

A follicle-thin light wave glimmered directly at him, and as he visualized his coordinates where the third eye could be found, he thought he heard a familiar burbling sound, such as an infant would make in refusing to accept a parentally guided spoonful of wholesome Pablum. Freddie soon realized that Cottonmouth had stealthily been following his every move. He now stood erect, leaning slightly over Freddie's shoulder, as they stared down at the gaunt figure of a man sprawled before them on the floor.

For a while Cottonmouth stood upright but realized he couldn't maintain this stretch of elasticity as his innards were aching, so he decided to view Yessie's corpse from a prone position on the ground. It was true he had loathed Yessie when he was very much alive, especially since Yessie had sought to buy him from Freddie for the purpose of skinning Cottonmouth and turning that scaly skin into strips of exotic high-end leather goods.

At the time, an enraged Freddie was on the cusp of selling Cottonmouth to Yessie because, in a jarring moment, his live-in companion had shredded Bruce, Freddie's snakish alpha tie. This unspeakable act of mayhem was witnessed by the lesser reptilian ties in Freddie's closet who hissed out their anguish and, from then on, suffered post-traumatic stress disorder.

Cottonmouth, now a more peaceable being, stared reflectively with glistening eyes at the corpse of his former adversary. It seemed to Freddie that an inward force, perhaps some residual love, inhabited Cottonmouth's guts, which couldn't be voided despite the best efforts of a brilliant herpetologist such as Dr. Copperhead. Taken aback by Cottonmouth's tears, Freddie couldn't believe that that very cold-blooded shingly critter, who shared his pillow night after night, was capable of displaying such warmth towards his bereaved compadre.

In his belief that the deceased could hear, Freddie struggled to find a few words of remembrance for one Yeshua Possumo, who had come to be known in the neighbouring bog land by the pet nickname, Yessie. For Cottonmouth, his attempt to eulogize Yessie was to emit a loud protracted hiss which rose up from deep inside him. Needless to say, it was far more difficult for Freddie to find the sorrowful words to grieve over Yessie's passing.

"Yessie," Freddie sputtered, "that crazy rotten bitch Laura assured me that you would come to no harm quaffing a bit of Fire Bull Surprise. I can see now that I am wrong. Can you forgive me?" Had Laura née Dewberry possibly sold him a bad batch of her special elixir that she concocted at Dr. Melon's mortuary? Hadn't she boasted that her pure products had sprouted hair as long as a heavy metal thrasher on the bald pate of a corpse she was working on? Freddie now arrived at the sad conclusion that Laura wasn't all that pharmacologically gifted.

There was no cognitive response forthcoming from Yessie, ne'er a dint of a natural blink, nor was there a spasm from Yessie's two über eyes now closed in a respectful repose. The third eye, however, was neither deaf nor dead as the rest of Yessie. Freddie was immediately put on his guard by a scornful glare emanating from the third eye. He deduced this phenomenon to be a radiating hateful light, a discharging source exuding from none other than Lucy.

Freddie would soon make short work of her and at the same time dispose of her hideaway vision seed. Still tenacious in his belief that his dead friend was aware of his presence, Freddie started gripping Yessie's stark white hands, squeezing those gelid fingers. It was Freddie's way of conveying his final goodbye to Yessie.

"Be at peace," Freddie whispered.

What transpired next astounded Freddie. His attention was drawn to Cottonmouth. Having sent his frenzied tongue flickering over Yessie's forehead, and then finding himself unable to offer a hardy sibilation of a farewell to Yessie, he jetted his tongue away from Freddie's brow.

Freddie realized that Cottonmouth had experienced a panic attack. But what has caused it? It didn't take him long to discover that the embedded Lucy in the third eye was beaming alarmingly at Cottonmouth, causing him, in his panicked state, to piss a slithering stream onto Yessie's face. The ring finger of Freddie's right hand quivered just as he muttered, "Granny, forgive me."

At once he plunged that precious spoon directly at the third eye, his mind going blank as a whoosh of blood exited. That blood flowed like a miniaturized pyroclastic flood from an eruptive volcano. And then it happened. Freddie's frizzy hair bristled in fear. Even his eyebrows shuddered, along with the whiffs of hair leading into nostrils, vibrating in sync with the enriched hairs in his wax-packed ears.

Yessie's parched lips began to stir. They seemed to beg for some liquid refreshment. Remembering Laura's boast that her fabulous concoctions could grow hair on bald cadavers, Freddie reasoned if that was possible perhaps then Fire Bull Surprise just might proffer a smidgen of life to Yessie.

On impulse, Freddie decided to pour the dregs of what remained in the glass of Fire Bull Surprise down Yessie's throat, but to accomplish this he had to force open his mouth, which wasn't easy, as rigor mortis had set in. Dr. Melon of the Gorgonia mortuary would have sold his mother platinum choppers to find that strong glue. It appeared to have more adhesive power than the Eternal glue he manufactured in his ghoulish lab.

Freddie, as luck would have it, found the crevice of an opening on Yessie's lower lip and managed to let a few drops of Fire Bull

Surprise slip into Yessie's mouth. Suddenly, Yessie popped open his eyelids, opened his mouth and shrieked "FFFFFFFffffffffffuck!"

Over and over again, in a *tich* of time, as life slipped away from him, he repeated his cussing mantra: "FFFFFFFffffffffffuck! FFFFFFFffffffffffuck! FFFFFFFffffffffffuck! FFFFFFffffffffffuck!"

More than a protracted death agony, it was Yessie's final liberating cry hurled at Lucy. She was now shrivelled up like a deceased ladybug inside a pod emptied of its mystical blood. It later became apparent to Freddie that so strong was Yessie's bond to his mother, that only death could free them both.

Holy Toledo!

The matter remained for Freddie of how to retain his dignity while disposing of Yessie's corpse. Having expressed his bereavement over Yessie's passing, rather than burying Yessie ignominiously in some mud flat of a nearby swamp and feeding a tribe of annelid worms, wasn't it better, mused Freddie, to offer Yessie's body to Handsome Harry instead to chow down on? But how was he to convey Yessie's body over to Handsome Harry's digs, where the offerings of former wise guys whacked on the orders of Tony Azazel were unceremoniously laid out as a fast-food snack for that prodigious gator?

Freddie realized that Yessie was the perfect meal for Handsome Harry. Yessie wasn't sartorially attired in any gator skin leatherwear, especially highly buffed Ferrini gator skin shoes to offend Handsome Harry's sensitivity. And further, Yessie carried no wristwatch, let alone some time piece that would be remotely akin to an indigestible phony knock-off Rolex, such as would wreak havoc with the big gator's gastrointestinal juices.

In life, Yessie was not one for conspicuous consumption, although he did on one occasion flash a blue enamel crucifix pendant with an antique gold finish.

When Freddie asked him where he had purchased that expensive crucifix complete with a silver neck chain, Yessie's eyes began to twitch.

"Somebody at the Pink Cygnet sold it to me," Yessie had blustered. "Yeah, it may have been Harry Longshanks who sold it to me, probably filched it from one of his ladies."

"That kid is no thief," Freddie had replied. "He has a shit load of money from pumping those rich bitches. Nah, he wouldn't be the type to go fencing a stolen crucifix just to buy a drink."

And it was true. Longshanks not only paid for his own drinks, but had often treated his friends to a round of tippling.

Freddie began to suspect that Yessie, as lay pastor of the Church of Yeshua, may have taken full advantage of his position in the church to liberate that crucifix from a member of the congregation.

Freddie, still bewildered by Yessie's sudden demise, hadn't noticed Cottonmouth's antics: his vibrato tongue seemed to waltz in sheer delight while trying to fit his yapper around the expired third eye, which passed effortlessly through the gates of his mouth.

"Holy Toledo!" bellowed Freddie. "Now you're done, you'll have the runs forever!"

Knowing full well Cottonmouth's preference for living food, Freddie then asked him how the third eye with its dead tenant tasted. How could he eat such a dreadfully deceased meal? He wasn't expecting Cottonmouth to reply, but he did just that.

"Yummy," he hissed, and suddenly Freddie realized that a resident evil being, living or dead, could indeed be a scrumptious feast.

Freddie's Request

How to dispose of Yessie's cadaver troubled Freddie and he turned to Cottonmouth with a request: could he summon his pal Handsome Harry, maybe invite the big gator over for lunch to chow down on Yessie? It seemed a reasonable request. Freddie knew that he and Hilda as canoodling couples would often joyride on Handsome Harry's back while that big guy drifted around the swamp.

"Ffffffff fuck off," hissed Cottonmouth, like Yessie's ghost, lashing his dominatrix of a tail at Freddie, indicating that he would have to kiss the very tip of his tail if he wanted to enlist his help in disposing of Yessie's corpse.

Freddie was prepared to accede to Cottonmouth's humiliating demand when the pillow suddenly rang in the bedroom, sending Cottonmouth skittering ahead to answer it, a call Freddie intuited could only come from Gabriel, possibly to rebuke him for having caused Yessie's demise.

Lashing his tail across the unmade bed, Cottonmouth plunged his snout deep into the pillow with hissing expletives, so obscene that the very fabric of the pillow turned fire-brick red, as though to convey the perception that the listener at the other end of the line was apoplectic with righteous anger, but after a few moments, the line went dead and the pillow returned to its natural colour, a soiled white which Freddie favoured.

"Now you've done it," squealed Freddie. "We'll both fry in that Lake of Fire if word ever gets out to his Boss that you sassed his number one messenger boy. I tell you, we're screwed and tattooed. Great jumping Jehoshaphat! Now why in blazes did you have to cuss Gabe out? Was it to pulverize me? Well, little buddy, you've done just that!"

Pleased with the irreparable damage he had caused Freddie, Cottonmouth tried his best to form a triumphant sneer, although the corners of his mouth ached because Freddie that morning had been particularly brutal in milking his venom. Still, Cottonmouth managed to form the same exultant grin he wore shortly after he had mangled Freddie's favourite snake tie, Bruce. Holding firm to his evil smirk, Cottonmouth gazed down at Yessie, baffled to see a sneer far more dominant than his forming on the lips of a supposedly dead man.

"Don't you fuss none, little buddy, that's rigor mortis completing its job and taking longer than it should with Yessie. What you're seeing now is what the guys in their white coats at the morgue in Gorgonia call Satan's Smile, and let me tell you there are a lot of grins going around these days."

Cottonmouth chortled in the way reptiles usually do and lashed his swinging tail in Freddie's direction.

"Kisssssss thisssssssssssssssss," he hissed, and in a voice more audibly human dispelled his sibilant phonetic English for Freddie's sake, allowing him to comprehend a viper's fluency. Not a hint of snake-accented English greeted Freddie's ears, as he got down on his knees to kiss the oscillating tip of Cottonmouth's tail.

"Tell you what," said Cottonmouth, with a haughty tone in his voice. "I'll invite Handsome Harry over for dinner. Now I want this stiff stripped naked and made ready for that eating machine. One other thing, you mud worm: get me a live fat rat. I don't fancy a deceased meal. Dead grub gives me gas."

In gratitude that Cottonmouth would assist him to dispose of Yessie's body, Freddie, with keen accuracy, planted a second kiss on the very same spot on the tip of Cottonmouth's tail, sending it gyrating into a vibratory mode of jubilation.

Please, Help Me

Cottonmouth felt he was clearly on the up and up in further plundering Freddie's self-esteem. He discovered, much to his delight, that he was in possession of a metastasizing vocabulary, although an odd one, with many of its words no longer in English usage. Nevertheless, he would use words in that strange dictionary to reproach Freddie for his poor personal hygiene, calling him, for instance, "a *slubberdegullion* of a man."

When Freddie demanded to know what he meant by that fifty-dollar word, Cottonmouth rose to his full tubular height and glared menacingly at Freddie, his forked tongue yabbering out of his mouth and vibrating in sync to his reply.

"Why, you got more filth on you than the local dog pound has fleas."

Taken aback by Cottonmouth's surly rejoinder, Freddie feared that too strong a rebuttal to his abusive rant would enrage him, and he'd then withdraw Handsome Harry's dinner invitation.

"Come closer, you piece of pusillanimous mouse turd!" stormed Cottonmouth.

"Puss at what?" exclaimed Freddie, finding the word unpronounceable, yet wanting to know its meaning. Feeling a little heat on his eyebrows, he was startled to find Cottonmouth's elliptical eyes staring directly at him.

"Before I invite my pal to dinner there are things I want," puffed Cottonmouth, putting on a warm smile to assure Freddie that he wasn't about to sink his fangs into him. But Freddie wasn't fooled. How often had he witnessed that same smile appearing on Cottonmouth's dark lips just before swallowing a squirmy rat, head first?

"I'll agree to anything you say," replied Freddie, backing away from Cottonmouth's probing eyes, "only help me get rid of Yessie's body."

"Say please," said Cottonmouth pursing his lips. "You never say please. Now that's just codswallop of the rudest kind."

"Very well," replied Freddie. "*Please,* help me get rid of Yessie's body."

"Okay, I will, but it will cost you something and you won't like it one bit."

Toothsome Beef

Testing to see if the corpse he viewed was truly dead, Cottonmouth slapped Yessie's face with the tip of his tail and soon realized that Yessie was as genuinely stiff as any corpse that Laura the mortuary artist beautified. Soon a glow of satisfaction covered Cottonmouth's face. It was a vengeful illumination for the man who once offered Freddie top dollar to buy Cottonmouth's skin; now it was Yessie ending up as a gob smacking meal for Handsome Harry. Cottonmouth, while relishing the thought of Yessie's devourment by that alpha gator, felt a yum yum gastrointestinal spasm coming on, followed by a line of involuntary drooling.

There was nothing more appealing to Cottonmouth's taste buds than inhaling a portly rodent, gradually swallowing his prey head first, and then, once the guts of that rat had twisted into liquid protein, Cottonmouth would take his mid-afternoon nap, having earned his rest after partaking of such a sizeable repast.

News had been leaked recently about massive out-of-state rats settling down in Freddie's neighbourhood and Cottonmouth had the hots to slurp down a few of those plump foreigners. If only Freddie possessed the skills in catching one of those free-range strangers for him to eat, he would then feel more at ease with Handsome Harry having his way with an unresponsive Yessie.

In his desperation to get Cottonmouth's help in disposing of Yessie's body, Freddie once again pressed his pallid lips against the very tip of Cottonmouth's tail, after which he acceded to Cottonmouth's wishes that he be allowed to take his pleasures with Hilda any time he saw fit. Yet, if this wasn't enough, Cottonmouth made a further demand: he wanted Freddie to wash the blemished pillow slip, its foul odour interfering with the love chemistry of his active pheromones mingling with the essential love perfume and the essential snake in Hilda. Freddie was too thick to realize that vipers like Cottonmouth were obsessive about cleanliness to the point of neuron meltdown.

If one is to go by the history of obsessive romance, then it could be said that romantics the likes of Cottonmouth shouldn't despair in facing an unsanitary environment, for true love with all its sighs, whispers, hisses and kisses can certainly block out the unsightly presence of feculent bedding.

Cottonmouth was careful not to overdo his conditions for assisting Freddie in disposing of Yessie's corpse, especially in demanding that Freddie do away entirely with those morning milking rituals. He feared that Freddie would be so taken aback by this demand as to instantly cancel Handsome Harry's dinner invitation.

In Cottonmouth's twisted mind, Freddie would be left with no other option but himself to undertake the enormous task of devouring Yessie, thus scratching out the power Cottonmouth currently possessed over him.

"Okay," said Cottonmouth sweetly, while managing to put on a most ingratiating smile which seemed out of place with the hostility glowering in his eyes.

"I'll get your damned dinner invitation out to Handsome Harry. But being the popular fellow around these parts, he may be completely booked up with far too many invites."

"Then he might not be able accept my dinner invitation?" Freddie whimpered.

Cottonmouth chuckled. "Nah, I'm sure he'll be available for this toothsome feast!"

A Darker Reason

Cottonmouth refused to allow Freddie entry into his dream. He didn't want to join him en route to Handsome Harry's stomping grounds. He alone would extend that dinner invitation on Freddie's behalf. But there was a darker reason for not having Freddie along for company: flashing his eighty plus teeth, Handsome Harry had indicated an interest to Cottonmouth in trying a chaw of Freddie, and upon finding his flesh succulent, he would drown him in a marinade of swamp water, and then begin scrunching his lifeless body into manageable mouth-size portions for an unforgettable nosh.

Cottonmouth didn't want to clue Freddie into that grim scenario since many a time he had contemplated asking his gator chum to chow down on Freddie, as then he would have had Hilda all to himself. Now, alas, she was currently involved with a flaming red-haired feral hog that some in the local pig hunting fraternity called Red Rufus.

She enjoyed pleasuring his awesome proboscis with nibblings of wet kisses, and he, being the reciprocal lover, returned her genuine affection in letting his tongue dance over the tiny topography of her dainty nose.

Cottonmouth assured himself that she was merely infatuated with that hoofer, and therefore their relationship was but a passing phase, but he wasn't about to tolerate any competition for Hilda, whether her lover walked on all fours, two legs, or slithered limbless like himself.

Would his chomping sidekick, he wondered, consider gulping down Red Rufus? There was a lot of meaty gristle on that snuffling hog. Handsome Harry had long ago acquired a taste for the odd gator hunter. How could he, a glutton extraordinaire, now turn down such a lavish feast?

Yet, unbeknownst to Cottonmouth, Handsome Harry's appetite had become jaded by gorging on heaps of whacked wise guys gifted to him by his benefactor and friend Tony, the Gorgonian crime boss, and now he yearned for a more challenging gustatory adventure, as any self-respecting predator in the wild might desire in approaching a *living* target of opportunity. *Perhaps this came from watching Freddie pursuing Hilda on her way to meet her oinker lover at some nearby hideaway?*

Cottonmouth and Handsome Harry, the best of confreres, possessed a unique way of communicating with each other, either in expansive hisses, or, from Harry, through a subtle play of cryptic hand signals. Poor Cottonmouth, being disadvantaged in having no limbs, could only rely on volumes of sibilation. Their camaraderie and arcane method of communication would have been the envy of every Masonic Lodge master.

Yet more remarkable, whenever they met on some mud flat or on a brackish waterway, Cottonmouth would charmingly peck a kiss on both sides of Handsome Harry's pointy proboscis to indicate his enduring friendship to the big gator.

So Cottonmouth's invitation for dinner was thunderously accepted with a growl, followed by a violent exhalation of air which rushed out of Handsome Harry's mouth. No thought, however, was given to the state of putrefaction of Yessie's corpse, or to its edibility. But it mattered little to Handsome Harry, who viewed a corpse's decomposition as a tenderizing catalyst in providing the nasty enzymes for a deplorably delicious meal.

A Triple Treat

It wasn't easy to entice Handsome Harry to accept a dinner invitation at Freddie's place. Cleverly, Cottonmouth knew the one thing that would please Handsome Harry more was clamping his jaws down on a serial gator killer, especially one who may have whacked his kin, so he fabricated a story how Yessie had once boasted to him how he enjoyed killing gators. Cottonmouth intimated to Handsome Harry that his mother may have been among the lot cruelly done in by Yessie.

A fast-moving confab followed between the two, with Cottonmouth promising Handsome Harry that an enticing dinner awaited him, worthy of any reigning marshland emperor, and a feast made tastier for Handsome Harry by the thought of him devouring the very man who may have murdered his mother. As Cottonmouth described the degree of decomposition of Yessie's corpse, the hues of decay on the flesh varying from a bluish grey to vibrant chartreuse. Their chat became more animated; ophidian hissings met a wall of sound in a gator's seismic rumblings and deep throat assibilation. And such was the depth and intimacy of their communication that it moved Handsome Harry to tears, for underneath that rough hide exterior was a mushy sentimentalist, although the thought of viewing a fast foodie in gastric heat chomping on Yessie's body chilled Cottonmouth's slow-food sensibility.

Handsome Harry, grumbling: "Sure, I'll be at the house. Is your mate joining us for dinner?"

Cottonmouth emitted a loud hiss: "No, but he said he would leave a juicy rat for me on the table."

Handsome Harry released a blast of noxious air: "Too bad, I was hoping to take a chaw of him."

Handsome Harry, his jaws opening wider: "I want a taste of him before I chew him up."

Cottonmouth grimaced: "I have someone you'll find a damn lot tastier, been dead awhile."

Handsome Harry, a slather of drool sliding from his lower jaw: "Yeah, that way, they're more scrumptious."

Cottonmouth, tongue flickering: "You don't say? Am I in for a double treat?"

Handsome Harry, a puzzled expression in his eyes: "So what's with this double treat?"

Cottonmouth, breathless at first and then exuberantly hissing: "This rat is pregnant!"

Handsome Harry gawping in amazement: "You mean she's a mother!"

Cottonmouth suppressing a chuckle: "Maybe a quadruple treat. Freddie said she was due for triplets."

Handsome Harry glaring at Cottonmouth: "You'd suck down a pregnant mother? Shame on you!"

Cottonmouth hissing his delight: "They're the best eating. I love it when they squeal inside of me."

Handsome Harry, stunned: "I'll settle for that stiff. But maybe you can give me a piece of her tail."

Gastric Heat

Handsome Harry trudged through the epic darkness of Cotton-mouth's dream until he arrived at Freddie's place. He didn't bother to knock but used the full force of his swishing tail and massive head to bash the door open, sending its hinges flying. Cottonmouth lurched forward and greeted Handsome Harry by planting a wel-coming kiss on both sides of his jaws. It was Cottonmouth's way of conveying his respect for his dinner guest. And it was indeed a can-dlelit affair. Before Freddie had taken off he had prepared the table, lit several candles secured in a silver candelabrum, laid Yessie's putre-fying body across the table, and bound a large grey rat to a plate using a special ligature which he had been taught as a Boy Scout; the rodent kept wriggling in terror, alternately squealing and fainting.

Of the two, Yessie could be said to be the lucky one. Being dead had some advantages. He wouldn't have to witness himself being ripped apart by a gator's serrated teeth, chewed and then devoured with the gusto of a thunderous gourmand who would waddle the extra mile just to gratify his gastric heat.

Handsome Harry's eyes shone like a child's eyes in a choco-latier's shop. He hissed and salivated over his supper.

"It smells delicious, ummmmmmmmmmmmmmmm. I think I'll go for a leg." He did just that and then, feeling a surge of visceral fire rising in his guts, tore off the other leg. Dragging Yessie's corpse off the dinner table, he slammed it hard in one easy motion onto the floor. It came apart as though it had been soaking in a mortuary marinade for over a century. Flaring out his tongue, Handsome Harry started licking the blood that spurted out of Yessie, and then with an inspired fury, itself poetry in motion, masticated those remaining limbs, flesh and bones soon minced together in an unholy matrimony.

"Eat heartily, my friend," hissed Cottonmouth, proceeding to swallow the rat, head first. A wild look of satisfaction appeared on

Cottonmouth's visage. Once again, he displayed the gentility of some good-mannered reptile. A quiet eater, taking a gourmet's pride in supping on slow food, he was never one to engage another diner in conversation. He turned his eyes away in disgust, a foodie snob unsettled by the frightful sight of a fast and furious eater.

Outside of what Handsome Harry viewed as inedible – gristles, tufts of hair, teeth and shards of bone stuck to splotches of congealed blood – nothing remained to identify Yessie. All Freddie had to do now after Handsome Harry left was to sweep up and bag the human remains. It troubled Freddie to think that he owed Cottonmouth a favour in return for helping him dispose of Yessie's body. But what perturbed him the more was his having to share Hilda with Cottonmouth. The thought of Cottonmouth putting the squeezies on Hilda gave him the hives.

Freddie, it was plain to see, was not only afflicted with twinges of jealousy, but feared that his rival for Hilda's affection would gratify her sexual needs, and consequently she would leave him for Cottonmouth. It was bad enough that she copulated with feral hogs, but what did she see in a cottonmouth? He didn't even have hands to hold her!

"Asphole," hissed Cottonmouth to Freddie, "that rat you left for me is giving me gas!"

Freddie shuddered to think that his buddy would now have premium carnal time with Hilda. He couldn't live with the thought of Cottonmouth pleasuring her. But he was a man of his word and a deal was a deal. Handsome Harry, thanks to Cottonmouth having persuaded him to accept a strategic dinner invitation, had taken care of the problem of disposing of Yessie's body by devouring it. And now Freddie would have to suffer the afflictions of jealousy in knowing Cottonmouth and Hilda would be making whoopee, and on his bed!

It was more than he could take. He even thought of using his pillow to call up Gabriel and ask for his divine intervention in preventing the pair's lusty entanglement. But in his heart he knew that Gabriel would have nothing to do with him, and further, what ruffled his dazzling feathers was Freddie's chumming around with Cottonmouth, whom the boss angel assumed was none other than Satan himself in a clever disguise.

Freddie realized he was on his own when it came to matters of the heart. Who was around to advise him about crashing on to the shoals of Tough Love? Some of the ne'er-do-wells at the Pink Cygnet Pub in Gorgonia would have counselled him to take a laxative and crap it all out.

Yet much to his surprise, far from being in turmoil, the little voyeur in him was warming up to the sight and sound of coupling lovers going at it with a steamy passion that would set both them and their bed on fire. From his bedroom closet he could observe the configurations of their lovemaking; his ties also eager to take in the view by peering over Freddie's shoulder. They bore a special animosity towards Cottonmouth, as their team leader, Bruce, had been torn to pieces by him in one of his more fitful rages. A soft rap on the door and Freddie knew the hour of true romance had finally arrived. He hastened into the closet just as

Cottonmouth sailed over to greet Hilda. Upon entering his digs, she extended her arms toward him and wriggled her hips.

Cottonmouth, having no hips, could only gawk at her, flare out his tongue, hiss and rattle the tip of his tail in jubilation. She was attired in a garb woven together with pampas grass, sundry aquatic leafage and white, yellow and red swamp orchids. The tight dress she wore served to enhance her curvaceous figure. It was an outfit very much favoured by Cottonmouth, for it brought out the undulant snake in her, especially on the horizontal.

A beam of light pierced through the darkness of Freddie's mind. He was a film mogul directing Hilda and Cottonmouth to act out a love scene, full bore. That scene alone would make the movie a box-office sensation. There, of course, would be a parental advisory warning, informing the public that this epic adult movie was not suitable for innocent eyes.

Sighs, Whispers, Hisses and Kisses

"Lights! Camera! Action!" the voice behind Freddie cried. One of his snake ties was getting boisterous. Leaning his triangular head over Freddie's shoulder, he emitted a piercing cry which reverberated in Freddie's ears.

"Cottonmouth, get your tongue in her groove. She's easy." Shocked by this salty outburst, Freddie pushed away Big Al, a brute of a necktie. A former confidante of the late Bruce, he now headed the pack.

"That's enough, ya hear? He doesn't need your coaching," Freddie grumbled, vexed by Big Al's sassiness.

"Back away, fellow – I'm the one who's directing this scene, not you!"

Big Al quickly pulled away from Freddie's shoulder, trailing a sperm-pale string of drool. Soon Freddie heard the other ties stirring. He sensed they wanted to get a closer view of the love scene unfolding on Freddie's bed. Cottonmouth's vibratory tongue was searching frantically for Hilda's God spot in an attempt to bring Hilda to a seismic orgasm, one that would rattle all his scales. Freddie was transfixed by the flickering movement of Cottonmouth's tongue. It seemed to have a life all its own, independent of the rest of Cottonmouth's elasticizing body. Freddie wasn't alone in his amazement at Cottonmouth's considerable amatory skills. Others were witnessing a tongue stud's poetry in motion.

It wasn't long before Freddie found himself holding back a crush of serpent ties. Lewd gurgling noises trickled into Freddie's ears while saliva trickled down the side of his neck. The neckwear horde with Big Al in the lead weren't about to be denied their viewing pleasure. Much to his surprise, far from being filled with jealousy as any man would watching his woman being serviced by another man, or beast – Freddie discovered that he was deriving an intense gratification in spying on Cottonmouth pleasuring Hilda, so much so, he hadn't stopped to realize that he, too, was salivating like those snake ties elongating over his shoulder.

Suddenly, Hilda emitted a cry so wild, that for an instant Freddie mistook it for a wounded animal. It terrified Freddie and especially his ties, a few of whom fainted and fell off their tie racks onto the closet floor.

"Yes! Yes! Yes! Ohhhhhhhhhhhhhhhhhhhhhhhhhhhhh." Hilda's body started to shake violently, rocking the bed with seismic delight. Cottonmouth's scales remained intact as Hilda experienced an orgasm that she could never ever hope to experience with any rutting feral hog, and certainly not with an ineffectual lover like Freddie.

From the closet, Freddie was audibly tuned into the commingling of sighs, whispers, hisses and kisses of the two lovers. On the quavering Richter scale of orgasms, Hilda had experienced one so intense that she thought she was going to expire, her life taken away on an updraft along with a tiny butterfly of shimmering silver, her fluttering soul.

An Alien Love Knot

The lovemaking between Cottonmouth and Hilda on Freddie's bed, as witnessed by the snake ties, seemed so wholesomely tender that they were instantly moved to tears. Big Al seemed particularly surprised. He wasn't one to weep. One couldn't say he was a sissified piece of neckwear, yet there he was, along with the rest of his associates, gushing tears, while cursing the artisan maker who had implanted a noxious sentimentality into his silken fabric. Had there been a contemporary Beau Brummell joining Freddie and his restive neckwear companions in the closet, he would have been immediately transfixed by a teary-eyed black-and-gold-striped creature that was so viperously Big Al in men's haute couture.

However, Freddie wasn't all that lachrymatory about his little buddy making it with Hilda. He appeared unsettled. Jealousy was getting the best of him. It wormed its way into his entrails and he was on the cusp of dashing out of the closet and separating the two lovers, when something frightfully out of the ordinary happened. It drew the very breath out of Freddie's body while at the same moment causing his necktie chums to undulate in fear and dribble pee. They could scarcely believe that what they saw was really taking place. Freddie assumed at first he was hallucinating. It often happened when he ate something that insulted his gastro-intestinal system, like a week-old partially eaten ham sandwich he found under his pillow which he had been saving for a bedtime snack, and had forgotten it was there.

Cottonmouth had been licking Hilda's erect raspberry-coloured nipples, causing her to groan, shiver and shake, and he was about to ride his manic tongue down to her pubic mound and plunge it past the inner labia into her moist darkness when Hilda, in the blink of an eye, turned into a creature partially reptilian. From the waist down, her legs having vanished, an extensible tail formed in its place. It swept across the bed, intertwining with Cottonmouth's tail, forming what Freddie perceived to be an alien love knot. Never in his Boy Scout days had he seen such a knot, certainly not one his queer scout master had shown him.

"Great Jesus Mongolian Christ," Freddie gasped. "I can't believe it!" He slapped both sides of his face in disbelief.

"Believe it!" cried the ties in unison. They were trembling, this time not in fear but in some gleeful delirium. Had Hilda metamorphosed into a snake queen worthy of being worshipped by them?

But Hilda's transformation turned out to be brief. In the shake of her tail, followed by a blinding flash of stardust, she returned to being the same wholesome Hilda of yore. She turned her head and stared directly into Cottonmouth's eyes. Her bright eyes bespoke of a supreme love.

"You're hot, baby, you're all mine," hissed Cottonmouth, wrapping his tail firmly around her middle and drawing her closer to his gaping mouth, exposing his fangs which appeared to grow in size. "You're mine," he panted.

"Yes! Yes! Yes!" she replied, spreading her legs. Cottonmouth knew instinctively that his gifted over-worked tongue was urgently needed to be pressed into service once again. He intuited correctly that no matter how many bowel movements he took (as once ordered by a brilliant herpetologist, Dr. Ricardo Copperhead), he would never expel the staggering amount of love stools buried in his eruptive guts.

Love's Perfect Unitary Circle

A few times in viewing Cottonmouth snuggling with Hilda as they relished their delectations, and maxing out on variations of love knots that suited Hilda's fancy when she morphed into an off-and-on-again snake woman, Freddie felt that he was on the verge of fainting. Big Al had to resort to sibilating comforting words into both his ears, not knowing if they were getting through the wax-packed canals. At the same time, the über-ties stroked his neck, and went about instinctively nibbling away at the right pressure points.

It worked to calm Freddie down. But it wouldn't last long. Unbeknownst to Freddie, Big Al had a twisty side to his personality. He was a snake tie with an imposing attitude problem, exhibiting features that some headshrinker would term a "dissociative disorder," one experienced by any individual having endured a traumatic experience, which in Big Al's case had very much to do with his witnessing Bruce being torn to pieces by a petulant Cottonmouth wanting to take his revenge on Freddie.

"I guess you're not man enough for that bitch," hissed Big Al. His derision called into question Freddie's sexual prowess, or the very lack of it. That hurtful diss was soon followed by a chilling cackle. It penetrated both of Freddie's ear canals, causing him to grimace in humiliation. There seemed nothing more debasing to Freddie than being bested by a bully such as Big Al.

"Go easy on him," churned the other ties. They attempted to do some damage control, assuring Freddie that Big Al didn't mean what he said, that he was only trying to liberate his blocked viperous masculinity and bring it to the surface; it was the natural thing to do for any male reptile trying to locate his mojo. Freddie, however, wasn't buying it. And then, to add further to Freddie's mortification, Hilda had once again morphed into a snake woman. Working the elasticity of her body to the limit, she managed to secure the tip of Cottonmouth's tail, gripping it firmly in her mouth as he, too, followed suit, locking his mouth onto the tip of her tail. Together they configured Love's perfect unitary circle.

As a hybrid of snake and woman, Hilda took her shamelessness to a lofty height. It stimulated her libido to know that Freddie was one of the closeted peepers. Cottonmouth gleefully watched her slide off the bed and head toward the closet where a pallid-faced Freddie stepped out to greet her. It seemed that all the blood in his face had drained out. It was though he had offered that vital sap to some deranged warlock in a satanic ritual.

Granny's Shoebox

What Freddie remembered before he fainted was the leer on Hilda's face. It was the type of leer that a naturalist would associate with a famished reptile about to pounce on a marsh rice rat for slow-food intake, and when Hilda went into a hissy mode and splayed her forked tongue, that was it for Freddie. He collapsed on the spot, while Big Al and his troupe of snake ties, their minuscule eyes frozen with terror, slipped from their closet hangers and collapsed on top of Freddie.

Their delicate hearts having burst, blood trickled from their mouths onto Freddie's grungy checkered shirt, staining it with the tiniest of red petals. Freddie knew that the shock of having countenanced the viper in Hilda proved too much of a shock for them, and that there wasn't as much as a drop left of Fire Bull Surprise to restore the lot back to life.

Teary eyed, he gently picked up the deceased, mumbled a few words of remembrance and interred his ties in an old shoebox which once belonged to his granny. What was unusual about that shoebox was its elevated shape, formed to accommodate his granny's club foot.

Freddie's attention was drawn to his bed. Cottonmouth and Hilda had left, but what he noticed amazed him. Either Cottonmouth or Hilda had sloughed off their skin! Had Hilda left a memento for Freddie? Was she no longer a snake? It seemed so eerie. But if there was a bipolarity of snake and sweet Hilda curved in all the right places, could she then possibly be venomous? It would mean milking her, squeezing out that venom, and that he couldn't do.

"Damn you," stormed Freddie. "What a ditzy slut she is. No regard for my feelings. I am not someone to be toyed with. It wasn't long ago when Cottonmouth played fetch with Hilda's dildo and now all I have to show for it is this snake skin!"

Freddie realized he was talking to himself. No matter. He didn't mind blathering to someone he enjoyed being with so much.

Addressing his shoebox, Freddie whispered, "I'll miss you guys, rest in peace. You have served me well."

The Sage Advice

Cottonmouth stayed less and less as Freddie's in-house companion, and when he occasionally did sleep over, Freddie would insist on extracting his venom before allowing Cottonmouth to bed down with him and share his half of the pillow. Freddie's insistence on milking Cottonmouth resulted in a brouhaha between them, with Cottonmouth slithering fast from Freddie's place in a terrible snit, leaving Freddie sulking in tragic solitude.

He started conversing with the only other being he could trust, himself, to receive the sage advice he desperately needed in confronting the raging jealousy eating away his innards like a famished tapeworm on steroids. It was plain to see that Cottonmouth was winning over Freddie in totally bewitching Hilda and becoming her numero uno beau.

In his mind's eye, Freddie could see the amorous couple joy-riding on Handsome Harry's back, titillated as the big gator drifted noiselessly through the murky waters of the swamp while keeping his eyes peeled for a tasty pink egret.

No longer that housebroken reptile, Cottonmouth had reverted to his natural, wild state. In his clouded brain, Freddie could imagine Hilda morphing time and time again into a snake. He watched Hilda intertwining her elongated lower body with that of Cottonmouth's elasticized tail, and together the enthralled couple would form a unified ligature of lust.

What Freddie feared most in that erotic configuration was the thought of Hilda's body bursting once she stretched too far past the elastic limit. But how was he to warn her of the carnal dangers of ligaturing with Cottonmouth when she rarely paid him a visit, and then again he knew the futility of reasoning with a woman who was too much in love, perhaps even of a fatal love bug infection. What he required now was some talk therapy. So he began to prattle loudly with himself, maxing out unsparingly on execrations. He could taste the bitterness in the invectives he would be directing against Hilda. Arsenic, the rat exterminator once told him, had the taste of bitter almonds.

"Yessie tried to warn me about her whoring ways, but I wouldn't listen!

"Freddie, you're right, she's always starved for serious sausage! Don't let her bend you out of shape. She's not your type."

"What do you mean, not my type? What kind of shitola is that?"

"Now don't get hot under your collar. You know exactly what I mean!"

"I do? What the fuck are you talking about? Lay off this crap."

"You know exactly what I mean...mixed betrothals never work out."

"Mixed betrothals? Sure, she's got her hang-ups, but we can work it out."

"Take the wax out of your ears...you're as thick as a fence post!"

"You can't talk to me that way, I've got dignity!"

"You had dignity once when you were a pup sucking on your momma's tit."

"Don't talk to me that way. If bullshit was music we'd have a brass band!"

"Now calm down or you'll blow a blood vessel. You don't look well."

"I'm well enough to take your insults, some friend you turned out to be."

"Don't you see that Hilda is part snake? How will the children turn out?"

"I can hatch those kids in their momma's eggs using an over-head heat lamp."

"Look, this is no joking matter. I am not amused by your levity. Give her up. She's a switch hitter. One minute she's Hilda, next, part viper."

"I guess you're right. You know this talk we had has done me good."

"You're feeling more like your own self then?"

"Better than that, old friend. I'm feeling like a pup on some dog run."

Dr. Copperhead had once put a weird notion into Freddie's noggin that babbling to oneself had been therapeutically effective with some of his more neurasthenic patients suffering from the most severe anxiety attacks. "Try hissing to yourself an hour a day for a month," the good doctor advised Freddie, "and you'll feel just fine. I should know. It damned well works for me."

The Stark Black Silhouette
of His Loneliness

Freddie found himself all alone. Cottonmouth no longer shared Freddie's abode or his pillow. Loneliness became Freddie's friend with whom he could while away the hours, grateful to have such a dedicated companion to share his dreams with. Unlike Cottonmouth, who greedily accepted the doctrine of the territorial imperative, Freddie's new-found bedmate wasn't at all pushy in gaining more of that pillow's terrain. Indeed, at times his loneliness would croon plaintively to Freddie: "I'm not crowding you off the pillow, am I?"

"Of course not," Freddie replied. "Thanks for your concern."

"You're more than welcome. Look for me in your dreams. Good night."

Cogitating on the ways of reptiles, Freddie concluded they were imperious creatures who meandered about sniffing out new territory. Like cats, they were natural empire builders. Gaining a selfless partner who tended to the needs of others before his own was truly a liberating experience. What a perfect mate, thought Freddie, simply the best. It moved him to tears. Noting Freddie's tears, Freddie's loneliness remarked, "Have I upset you somehow?"

"Oh no, I'm just so happy to have you around."

"I'm honoured to be in your company," his loneliness beamed.

After a while, Freddie found that he could do without his "little buddy," as he was wont to call Cottonmouth. Freddie felt relieved in knowing he would no longer have to deal with the morning ritual of extracting Cottonmouth's venom, but how could he squeeze out the thought in his head that Cottonmouth had run off with Hilda, for if ever jealousy was a tapeworm, Freddie's parasite was ineradicable, lodged in his darkest moss pit of a heart.

"Damn, I miss her. I really do. What does she see in Cottonmouth?"

"Freddie, I believe she has been hypnotized by that no good viper."

"You're right. Why, I've seen him freeze a rat with those eyes!"

Freddie was being eaten away from the inside out. Something had to be done to kill that wriggler! It was time to go on the offensive: locate Hilda, drag her away from whatever rutting beast she was involved with, but more importantly, Cottonmouth would be put in his place. He would have Cottonmouth playing fetch as before. If it wasn't a dildo to be fetched it would be Freddie's tattered socks or ragged boxers.

He planned to track Hilda down and talk some sense into her, and with patience, there was a chance of rekindling their old romance.

In the throes of their lovemaking he would be on his guard. He would spring away from her the very instant she changed into a partial snake and attempted to lunge at him and nip him fatally in the neck. Once again Freddie took cognizance of Dr. Copperhead's warning. There was toxicity in the highs of love which had to be crapped out lest it attack and corrode the body's vital organs.

"Freddie, she'll come back to you. She's just infatuated with Cottonmouth."

"Infatuated, that's it! You're right. Thanks for helping me out here."

"Don't mention it. She still has the hots for you. Be patient and loving."

Thanks to his friend counselling him on the matters of the heart, Freddie became convinced that a wee blush of love was still vibrantly on the rose. But first there was the matter of following up on the leads where she and Cottonmouth were last seen by a few of the locals.

He was mulling over his tracking stratagem to locate the pair when the telephonic pillow rang in the bedroom. It had to be

Gabe calling, thought Freddie, for who else knew his private number? He hurried over to answer his pillow and when he did he heard what he assumed to be the clap and roar of thunder in the background. This he took as chain lightning. But after a moment or two the line was clear:

"Hello, hello out there, is that you, Gabe?"

"Don't call me Gabe. You are to address me respectfully as Gabriel!"

"Don't get sore now, Gabriel. Have you any messages for me?"

"I have, you lump of protoplasm! My Master is displeased with you."

"How so, I've done nothing wrong...have I?"

"Yes, you most certainly have done something terribly wrong!"

"Now what have I done to displease the Maker?"

"It's that foot-loose strumpet of yours cavorting with Satan!"

"Gabe...Satan? You're not inferring that Cottonmouth is Satan?"

"Now, how many times have I have told you not to address me as Gabe?"

"I mean, Gabriel, Don't get sore. It won't happen again, Gabriel."

"Your whore is cavorting with Satan and fornicating with swine."

"She is? Well, how do you know that? Have you located her?"

"Your whore has given my Master a stye. He has caught her in the act!"

"And what act may that be? Am I to assume she is making it with a hoofer?

"Yes, she is engaged in an unsightly and most vile act of zoophilia!"

"Zoo what? Now, that sounds real bad, I reckon, whatever it is."

"My Master is concerned about the well-being of that wretched swine."

"You don't mean that Tiny John is in some kind of danger?"

"My Master has detected some heart fibrillation in your Tiny John."

"If you give me his coordinates I can track him down and warn him."

"He'll have to cease coupling with that whore. She's killing him!"

"Hello, hello...the line is going dead...are you there, Gabriel?"

Freddie's pillow transformed back into a normal soiled cushion for the noggin. Freddie went into the bathroom and stared at his image in the mirror. Sensing the presence of someone in the back of his head, he quickly turned around only to glimpse at the stark black silhouette of his loneliness.

Four Eyes Are Better than Two

Had Freddie known what lay in store for him he would have abandoned his quest to find Hilda. But love as a troubling disease can't be entirely voided, for always some residue remains, which can launch a lover along the wrong pathway, straight into the gristly jaws of Fate. Lovers by the score have been masticated in this fashion, until all that remains of them is an oozing pulp spiked with fragments of bone detritus and hair follicles.

Unbeknownst to Freddie, Cottonmouth had made a pact with Handsome Harry to have Freddie killed. He knew Handsome Harry drooled at the thought of chowing down on Freddie. It was a perfect arrangement for Cottonmouth. His main rival for Hilda would be bumped off; and as for that bit player Tiny John, Hilda's tusked lover (rumoured to be the martyred Porco Pete's half-brother), he ended his days served up as a snack for Handsome Harry, much to Cottonmouth's delight, who witnessed the gustatory performance.

The news of Tiny John's demise, however, didn't sit well with Hilda. Upon hearing the news of how Tiny John had been so monstrously dispatched, she fainted. Cognizant of Hilda's fragile sensibility, Cottonmouth was determined that she wouldn't learn of his plan in having Freddie eliminated. Almost swooning at the prospect of Freddie being devoured, Cottonmouth discharged a protracted hiss in his compadre's direction. That assibilation was the reptilian equivalent of a promissory *bon appétit*, to which Handsome Harry responded in kind by expelling a stupendous volume of intestinal gas through his mouth to convey his gratitude to Cottonmouth for setting up Freddie as the long sought-after meal he craved.

"Must you go looking for Hilda?" chirped Freddie's loneliness.

"Yes, I must," Freddie responded. "I am hooked on her."

"Seems like you've got it bad. You don't look good."

"I must have her back. I can't live another day without her."

"Let me help you find that woman of your dreams!"

"Sure could use your help. As I always say, *four eyes are better than two*."

Mother, Mother, Is it Really You?

Freddie and his loneliness wandered past the familiar swamp lilies, their splayed white floret tongues greeting the pair, and as they passed by, the nocturnal sweet one-note trills of song sparrows filled the musty air to accompany the ghostly will-o'-the-wisps flaring in the darkness.

The evening was filled with the sweet smell of swamp roses intermingling with the delicate fragrances of pond apple, myrtle and other wetland floral aromas, and as though inebriated by inhaling that plant life, swarms of fireflies could be seen swarming into the darkness, their flashing tails being slowly extinguished, as though the evening itself had quietly devoured them.

"We're walking into a trap!" Freddie's companion suddenly blurted out.

"What's this trap you're yapping about? Are you a yellow-bellied wussy?"

"Don't call me yellow. I smell danger at the end of this trail, big danger!"

"Danger?" replied Freddie, mocking the namby-pamby in his loneliness.

"Damn you! Clean the wax out of your ears. They're waiting for us!"

"Who's waiting? You're hysterical, that's what you are, and yellow too!"

On a hunch, Freddie deduced that his loneliness was on the verge of a hysterical breakdown, and having watched forties' and fifties' film noir movies (being a junkie of that film genre), he decided a good slap was the only way to bring calm to a hysterical subject, and so he did just that, slapped his loneliness hard across the face.

Freddie, however, didn't take into account that all those freaked-out victims in those old movies were women, not hard-ass macho guys – usually private detectives who enjoyed having svelte women around as clients. Their "dames" were usually weak-kneed blondes desperately in need of serious slap therapy. The shock therapy, however, didn't go over that well with his loneliness, for as if by magic a frightful upraised red welt appeared on his right cheek.

Freddie soon realized that he had blown any glimmer of hope in having a potential soulmate accompany him in his quest to locate Hilda.

"Why did you do that? You're crazier than an old coot. I'm splitting."

"Please don't take it personally. I had to snap you out of your hysteria."

"You can piss up a tree with your hysteria, if you got the right pressure."

"Don't leave me," Freddie pleaded. "I'm begging you—"

Freddie's pleading proved in vain as the embodiment of his loneliness vanished, only to reappear moments later as a grinning half-formed apparition, whose face looked very much like Freddie's but healthier and more robust. Yet even ectoplasm has a short shelf life, for soon it disintegrates, crackling static electricity, not of this world.

Freddie reached out to touch the remaining particle charges. They swirled about him like fireflies showing their off-and-on-again incandescence. With his loneliness having abandoned him, Freddie began to wonder if his head had been improperly wired from the outset. Had he been talking to himself? There was the presence of a bruise on his right cheek which was now aching, suggesting he was the sole recipient of that slap. He was never partnered to a being he called his loneliness. Hilda, in deserting him in favour of Cottonmouth, had reduced him to a delusionary state. Some alien force had been making an attempt to appropriate his corporeal body. Yet, he still was not completely out of the psychic woods, for soon he involuntarily started mumbling to himself, and what was worse, the volume was too low, not on the right frequency.

He could barely make out what he was saying. Yet it didn't seem to matter. A thin-sounding radio voice inside his head was telling him that it was now up to the bona fide Freddie to track down Hilda and wrest his darling away from Cottonmouth.

He would continue his trek first thing in the morning, confident that no harm would come his way as he approached the hideaway thicket where he knew Hilda and Cottonmouth often used to carry on their amorous trysts.

Feeling drowsy, Freddie decided he would get some shut-eye. He lay down on the mossy ground beside the trunk of an ancient willow tree, and nearby spotted the perfect headrest which only nature could provide in the form of a morbidly obese fungus, a giant puffball, the size of a basketball, but the exterior of that phenomenal fungus, being firm and spongy, proving superbly pillow-worthy.

"Thank you, Lord," whispered Freddie, "for the making of this pillow."

Freddie yawned, and falling asleep, drifted into the interior of an alabaster cloud which opened to welcome him in. It was moist, warm and furry inside. He had a feeling that he had been there before. It was so damn comforting resting his weary head on that pillow, a gentle white light bathing his eyelids. Never had he known such tranquility; the silence was almost unbearable.

"Mother, Mother, is it really you?" chirped Freddie.

Let's Find My Whore

Freddie awoke the following morning, startled to find he was staring at a colossal silvery butterfly which had alighted on his chest. Freddie guessed that his ghostly visitor, whose wingspan he estimated to be five or more inches, was some type of alien eye-candy, a cut above the regular lepidopterous set. It tempted the effete boys in their noiseless soft canvas shoes to push through the pampas grass with their aerial insect nets to nab this dazzling trophy of a lifetime, adding that pulchritudinous flutterer to join other overdressed butterflies and moths pinned to some foam-board necropolis inside the sarcophagus of a glass-covered display box.

Yet, to Freddie, this critter seemed like no earthly butterfly, a lost spirit perhaps, or even some newly departed person's soul.

Freddie was even more shocked to discover that the countenance of this magnificent insect he was ogling appeared to be keeping him under surveillance. He closed his eyes, hoping that the instant he opened them this prodigious butterfly would instantly vanish.

But there it was, still on his bosom, boldly flapping its wings in defiance. It seemed to Freddie that they were combatants in a test of willpower, as to who would be the first to be spooked out. Freddie soon began to realize that his resolve to beat his opponent was waning, and to his surprise he found himself suddenly extending an arm out to the critter, which then flew onto the back of Freddie's hand. Freddie found himself in a tête-à-tête situation as he ventured to have a closer look at the object of his curiosity.

"It can't be, I must be dreaming," quipped Freddie, straining his eyes at what he perceived to be the teensiest face on that magnificent insect, and a face distinctively human! So frightful an experience was it for Freddie that, had there been some dream cumulous drifting by, he would have instantly jumped in, preferring entombment in some maternally warm interior than confronting the cold exterior reality of that butterfly's immense vibratory wings.

Freddie was on the verge of shooing away his visitor when, to his amazement, it started talking, not in the jabbering lingo which only a top-flight entomologist could decipher but in English, although on a low frequency: "Don't you recognize my voice? Bend an ear closer to my mouth."

"What mouth? I can't see where your mouth is," responded Freddie testily.

"No need to use that nasty tone of voice on me. I'm not some dung beetle."

"Okay, you freak, I'm close enough. I say turn the volume up."

"Pull the wax out of your ears, 'cause I'm a dude reborn, a soul you might say."

"You can't be Yessie. He got chewed up real good by some mean-ass gator."

"Have a closer look, pal, and then tell me if this isn't my kisser."

"Hot damn!" chirped Freddie. "Your puss hasn't changed at all."

"It hasn't? Are you sure? Something just doesn't feel right with my mug."

"Why, you're much healthier looking and your eyes aren't twitchy."

"I'm free of Mother," warbled Yessie. "I'm one heck of a happy traveller."

"So where's your dear old mom? Has she turned into some cockroach?"

"Don't go cussing Mother! Listen up; Cottonmouth has set a trap for you."

"Then you've seen my Hilda? Is she with that creep, Cottonmouth?"

"Yes, I have seen them together, making out like there was no tomorrow."

"Will you help me find her? I will make it worth your while."

"Make it worth my while? My proboscis only sucks up the juiciest nectar."

"Consider it done. Your soul food will be the sweetest honey-suckle nectar."

"In that case I'll just have to tag along with you to find your whore."

In a flash, Yessie fluttered up onto Freddie's shoulder and, using it as a roost, stood there rattling his wings as though to convey an impression that he was suited to his new role as Freddie's minder, and thus duty-bound to enlighten him in the ways of God's love and in His goodness, while prevailing on Freddie not to seek the false love of some shape-shifting strumpet who gratified her sexual appetite by cavorting with rutting wild boars and being carnally ligatured to a low-life such as Cottonmouth, shamelessly begging for more of his compressions, until her body rocked and rolled orgasmically, and then melded snakishly with his snakishness.

"Mother says her kind end up flamed for eternity in the Lake of Fire."

"No more preaching, you hear?" yowled Freddie. "Let's find my whore."

Skipper, Be My Eyes in the Sky

As Freddie moved along the pathway leading to where he hoped he would meet up with Hilda, he feared that Yessie, his spiritual essence now mineralized into a large butterfly, might awaken from a nap and excrete a stool of vile poop on his shoulder if, indeed, Yessie in his present state possessed bowels or, for that matter, a bladder to relieve himself. It seemed ridiculous to Freddie to imagine that a mere butterfly, even one as awe-inspiring as Yessie was, could carry out those bodily functions of a superior being like himself. Freddie gloated at his pre-eminence over Yessie.

"Do you need to do a dump?" said Freddie brusquely, with a commanding voice that shook Yessie out of his reverie and sent his wings aflutter.

"Dump, dump," mumbled Yessie, partly asleep and yawning like a newborn.

"Damn you! Do you need to take a crap, you know, a shit?"

Incensed by the insolence in Freddie's tone of voice, Yessie flew off Freddie's shoulder onto the bridge of Freddie's nose, fanning his wings in anger.

"I'll have you know I don't approve of that kind of language."

"I'm sorry that I offended you."

"Apology is accepted. Let's be on our way. I'll fly ahead."

"You haven't eaten all day. You must be starved."

"A dab of pollen will do, thank you, if we see a patch of milkweed."

"There are some orchids straight ahead filled with refreshing nectar."

"I can sure use a drink. I need to fuel up. We have a long way to go."

"Let's be off then. Do your reconnoitering, Skipper, be my eyes in the sky."

In Denial

Every once in a while, Yessie's spiritual envelope would hover over a multi-flowered Ghost Orchid, and send his thready proboscis in for a vertical dive deep into the narrow cradle of that orchid to suck up some energy enriched-nectar. The capillary action revitalized Yessie even as it turned him into a happy, devil-may-care tippler leaping jubilantly about in an aerial ballet.

"Tastes so heavenly," moaned Yessie, his antennae sniffing for other floral fragrances.

"Hey, stop your boozing," cautioned Freddie. "You'll bust a gasket if you don't stop."

"I'm feeling so good, can't stop. The more I drink, the more I want."

Yessie's imbibing seemed to be getting the better of him, and it wasn't just his viewing every orchid as a potential watering hole which troubled Freddie.

Freddie was shocked to see Yessie moving in on some liquid deposits of excrement left on a leafage of wet ferns by some loose-bowelled animal. Freddie, who didn't go in for "fifty-dollar words," wouldn't have known what coprophagia meant, for being your average Joe, "shit eater" would just have easily sprung off his lips, and science not being Freddie's shtick, he didn't much care that some feces provided nourishment for fungi, beetles and even butterflies.

How could something so beautiful and as pristine as Yessie's soul transmuted into a butterfly get hammered on feculent high-balls? It baffled Freddie and threw him for a loop. Now, he could understand dogs wolfing down their own shit. Many a time he had seen his blind pit bull Snarlowe use his gifted snout to locate some fresh stool seasoned with flies.

"Gads, your breath smells like Satan's arse," stormed Freddie, plugging his nose.

"But it tastes just like that orange blossom honey I had yesterday," pleaded Yessie, shaking his wings, signalling for Freddie to join him at his open kitchen. To his dismay, Freddie began to realize that the particles of goodness and grace which had gone into transforming Yessie's spirit into an object of pulchritude had somehow become corrupted.

"You're a shameless souse," Freddie crackled. "What would your momma say?"

"I must keep my energy level going," replied Yessie testily. "I need to juice up."

"If you keep on stopping for a shit drink," snarled Freddie. "we'll never find my Hilda!"

Vexed by Freddie's intemperate language, and in no mood to be reproached in such a disdainful manner, Yessie began to levitate, and in seconds flat, landed on the saddle of Freddie's nose, and not for the usual ophthalmic voltage of encounter which cow-eyed couples, smitten by the love disease, often display.

Freddie, although he wasn't aware of it at the time, was being triangulated by Yessie's compound eyes into triangular-shaped Freddies, scorn in every one of Yessie's multiple gazes. Yet what Freddie's eyes perceived, and what burrowed into his mind, was the realization that Yessie's soul was in denial of his addiction.

A Drunken Soul

With his besotted aide collapsed on his shoulder like a drunken noodle, Freddie started on his way to find Hilda. Had any man other than Freddie known what lay in store for him, he may have brushed that souse of a soul off his shoulder as so much offal, turned about and hastened home, but a man so hopelessly in love as Freddie was willing to face all manner of danger for the woman he loved.

"Hey, what's that pretty thing you're hauling?" a voice snickered deep inside Freddie's head, repressing what sounded like a derisive laugh.

"Is that you, loneliness?"

"Why are you toting that barfly on your shoulder?"

"That's my scout you're talking about. He's a bit stoned on nectar."

"Some scout you have there. Get rid of that good-for-nothing lazy freak"

"That lazy freak happens to be the precious soul of a friend of mine."

"What good is he if he can't do any scouting for you? He's just a boozer."

"Look, he's taking in some energy fuel to do some reconnaissance for me."

"Take it from me, chum, I know a drunken soul when I see one!"

"Damn you! Get out of my head! Vacate the premises at once!"

And his loneliness did exactly that. He was gone in an instant. Freddie then turned to see if his divine passenger hadn't become unsettled by the angry exchange between him and loneliness. Fortunately his "scout" appeared to have slept soundly throughout that ruckus, but for Freddie there was little in the way of tranquility. He became increasingly agitated as he realized he had to get a move on if he was going to wrest Hilda away from Cottonmouth's mad grasp.

"Turn back! Turn back! That whore isn't worth dying for!"

"I thought I told you leave my head alone, now be gone!"

"I'm only considering your well-being, no need to get pissed off with me."

"I say get the fuck out of my head!"

"Just warning you, that's all I'm doing. Goodbye for now, sucker!"

Being physically challenged in not having the hands to hold Hilda the way a woman ought to be held, Cottonmouth had resorted to turning his entire tubular body into an expanding and contracting apparatus, a love muscle, which when properly ligatured around Hilda's waist, and with just the right pleasurable compressions applied, would induce Hilda to ululate like a she-wolf in heat, each *petite mort* lofting her to paradise, and then back down to earth for a soft landing. Freddie wondered what his chances were of pulling Hilda away from the grasp of Cottonmouth's love muscle.

"Oh, yes! Yes!" Hilda squealed in his memory. "Feels so good, more please, more!"

Freddie closed his eyes, and after a moment or two erased the garish scene he had once witnessed when spying upon the pair making out in their hideaway.

Suddenly, Freddie's "scout" flew off his shoulder, hovered for a moment above Freddie's head, flapped its wings and sailed away, duty-bound as Freddie's eye in the sky, to report back to him on what dangers lay ahead for Freddie. How could he go wrong, Freddie mused, with such a splendid scout working on his behalf?

"She'll come to her senses once I have her on my bed," he mused.

"Don't count on it, pal," a voice trilled in his psyche before fading away.

"I'll get her back. I know I will," Freddie replied.

Yet, what Freddie hadn't taken into account was the reptile's uncanny intelligence. Not that Freddie was bereft of any intelligence, but he wasn't at all the brainiac that Cottonmouth was, nor could ever hope to be.

Not one to let the swamp grass or moss grow under his belly, Cottonmouth applied his smarts to having Freddie rubbed out, thus drawing Hilda under his sway as her principal lover and sovereign ruler. And so once again he found himself approaching Handsome Harry with a request. It was one that the big gormandizer couldn't possibly ignore, and Cottonmouth knew it.

Cottonmouth planted an obsequious kiss on both sides of Handsome Harry's cheeks before he explained the purpose of his visit, and immediately, as expected, received Handsome Harry's full attention. Cottonmouth had lost count of how many times Handsome Harry had expressed a desire to chow down on Freddie. As there wasn't quite the meat hanging on him as on some of the obese mob hits, Handsome Harry's desire puzzled Cottonmouth. Why would he fancy a scrawny prey like Freddie, at most a minimalist meal?

Had Handsome Harry become increasingly health conscious, indulging in a diet of lean fat-free beef? Perhaps too many helpings of mob stiffs had made him feel lethargic, even slothful. Somehow he had to get the weight off if he was to lunge and take down a stocky hoofed wild hog.

Most recently, Handsome Harry, to his horror, had found that one of the corpses he was set to demolish belonged to his benefactor and friend, Tony Azazel. Out of respect for Tony, he passed on eating him, and with tears leaking from his drooping eyes, decided instead to give him a decent burial under a nearby mud bank.

In blissful innocence of Cottonmouth's rabid plan, Freddie was attending to the passage of his scout, waving at that spirit soaring high above him, doing aerobatic manoeuvres, double loops, wings aflutter...

"Skipper," bellowed Freddie, "you're on the job, good for you!"

The Bird Who Had an Artist's Eye for Beauty

High above Freddie, a black-and-white-coloured Swallow-tailed Kite, its forked tail fluttering in the open kitchen of the sky, was making the rounds searching for nourishment when it spotted what was unmistakably a large white butterfly.

Freddie looked on helplessly as Yessie's soul tried to out-manoeuvre an agile raptor, a ballet of death with only one win-ner. It wasn't going to be his skipper. In seconds, that graceful predator sailed away with its prey firmly clenched in his beak, a whack job over in a blink of a predator's eye.

"Goodbye, skipper," wailed Freddie, scrubbing tears from his eyes.

It seemed so unreal. Only an hour before, Yessie's eye in the sky had brought Freddie valuable reconnaissance information. Hilda and Cottonmouth had been spotted in their usual hideaway, but what Freddie didn't care to hear was his skipper's graphic account of the coupling pair's intimacy, their lovemaking borne out in squeezes, hisses and tongue-to-tongue lavishings followed by a graveyard silence, signalling the completion of mutually sat-isfying sex via a ligatured configuration, perhaps a 69?

"No more, no more, I don't want to hear any more," gasped Freddie, who detected a grin on the infinitesimal face of that smarmy butterfly waving his antennae, wondering if Yessie's soul was suffering from a dementia caused by sucking up far too much nectar combined with an abundance of feces. No doubt about it, Freddie declared to himself, souls are not only tipplers, they're also shameless shit eaters!

"Stop, I don't wish to hear any more!"

"But I haven't told you the good part."

"Shut your yap!" howled Freddie at his tormentor circling above him.

The phenomenal butterfly kept ascending, and as it did, Freddie noticed that its colour was changing. From a bright titanium white, it turned a silvery hue, and then shifted to a florescent yellow. Yet, the latter colour proved fatal to Yessie's soul, for it was that very colour, in sharp contrast to the backdrop of a cerulean blue sky, which attracted the bird that had an artist's eye for beauty.

A Gruesome Steak Tartare

As Freddie went on his way, more determined than ever to get his luscious Hilda back, he felt that someone nearby was following him. He turned about and what he saw made him shudder. It was his shadow, and Freddie didn't care for the company.

"Why in the hell are you following me?"

"I'm not following you. I'm your better half."

"Oh, you are, eh? You don't by chance suck on nectar, or eat shit?"

"Look, no need for that kind of foul language. I'm here to warn you!"

"Warn me? Warn me about what?"

"Handsome Harry is waiting to bushwhack you."

"My skipper didn't see any king-size gator lying about."

"Your skipper didn't see that bird coming at him, did he now?"

"Okay, you made your point. So where is Handsome Harry?"

"He's lying there in the sawgrass, taking in the sun."

"Well, he can keep on sunning himself while I find my Hilda."

"You're a damn fool! Terminally stupid!"

"Turn around,. Mister Badass Shadow, and don't you follow me again."

"Alright, I'll leave you to your peril. Yeah, kiss your ass good-bye!"

In less than a blink of an eye, Freddie's shadow vanished. It sent a chill down Freddie's spine, giving true meaning to the often heard phrase of being scared of one's own shadow, which Freddie undoubtedly was.

Yet this shadow tailing Freddie was somehow different. Not only could it talk, it cared enough about Freddie to warn him of a sun-loving gator who desired to make a gruesome steak tartare out of him.

Soon Freddie pondered some dire reflections; perhaps he should have accepted his shadow's companionship when it was offered, but where had his better half gone? Was it too late to beckon him to return?

Waiting for Freddie to stroll by, Handsome Harry rolled over on his back, and as he did, his jaws opened and closed and eighty teeth locked neatly together, but not before a stream of saliva flowed down his massive chest.

A Grotesquery of Violence

Freddie looked up toward a powder-blue sky and thought he heard the mournful baying of his long-departed pit bull, Snarlowe. Ever the faithful companion, vigilant in protecting his master, he was ululating to Freddie, cautioning him to go no further.

In Snarlowe, Freddie sensed a gifted psychic, remembering how he had once blocked his master from continuing his stroll on a nature trail overlooking a patch of wet land, and a good thing he did, for a juvenile gator lay crouched in the pampas grass, waiting to leap out and take a wholesome chunk out of Freddie.

"Snarlowe, you silly mutt," intoned Freddie brusquely, "not you, too?"

Snarlowe replied with a few piercing barks followed by a yip.

"Snarlowe, where are you, my furry friend?" said Freddie, scratching his brow, as Snarlowe vanished from sight, and yet he could feel Snarlowe's long, flexible tongue leaving a deposit of drool on his pant leg.

"Where have you gone?" shrilled Freddie. "Back to your dog run in the sky?"

No response issued from Snarlowe, ne'er as much as a whimper. And yet he felt Snarlowe's spirit was nearby watching over him, vigilant in protecting him from harm. Still, not having that full-bodied Snarlowe at his side as he set out to find Hilda put him in a cobalt-blue funk.

Hurrying along in his aim of repossessing Hilda, Freddie suddenly became aware of the hum of incandescent electrical charges encircling his neck, and then gasped in disbelief as a ghostly tie with a distinctive viper's head came into view.

"Bruce, is that you?" queried Freddie.

"Turn back, danger ahead, please turn back," whispered Bruce, pressing his tongue into Freddie's ear. But before Freddie could express his joy in seeing Bruce, he vanished like the slithery smoke from a fog machine.

Freddie wondered if he had experienced the whole whammy of a hallucination or just the essential electro-chemical particles which go into the making of a vibrant delusion. He began to sigh in his disappointment.

If only he could have worn Bruce as an item of ectoplasmic neckwear one final time!

And yet, had he been as psychic, as he claimed Snarlowe was, he would have instantly turned about and hightailed it back home, for he would have witnessed a grotesquery of violence such as he had never seen before.

In contrast to dining out and enjoying a meal, one which Cottonmouth could leisurely devour at a snail's pace, Handsome Harry, charging at his prey in a white heat, would have out-sped the fastest magnetic levitation train on any rail on earth, which for Cottonmouth begged the question: did his pal get a rush of absolute succulence in his haste to demolish his prey? Cottonmouth abhorred a fast eater but made a rare exception when it came to Handsome Harry's unsophisticated style of victualing.

Freddie wasn't just challenged as a psychic, that gift being a rarity among humankind, his situation was made all the more perilous in his remaining oblivious to the dangers that lay ahead because of the accumulation of toxic love feces in his system. Freddie had been warned by Dr. Copperhead to "let go of that half-reptilian strumpet," but she continued to cling to his poisoned psyche like a bullwhip on a tomato.

A Proper Blood-Hued Drenching

Hours before, Handsome Harry decided to lie down in the pampas grass and bide his time waiting to ambush Freddie. He had just finished demolishing the controller of the moss pit gang. What Handsome Harry failed to notice was the significance of the moss stuffed into the controller's mouth, implying that the shooter was indeed a moss pitter. No, what counted for that gorger was the sudden rush of succulence he relished in noshing on a bloody flank of raw meat, free of the bristles as one would find on a body of a wild boar.

Handsome Harry found parts of the controller's corpse indigestible, but what especially wreaked havoc with his digestive juices was the controller's moppish hair, particularly the wild calligraphy in the curlicues of his lengthy beard which caused Handsome Harry to later cough up copious amounts of fur balls.

Cottonmouth had lost count of how many times he had to urge Handsome Harry to slow down and enjoy his meal one leisurely bite at a time and take a moment to reflect on the mouthwatering grub he was eating. But it proved an exercise in futility for Cottonmouth, as even he could not quell the mindless heat and primal fury of an appetite which knew no bounds in a fast chow down.

At that moment, an acute olfactory receptor in Handsome Harry's mouth picked up a whiff of Freddie's scent, and immediately his body tensed into an attack position, feet readying to spring off the ground, prepared to zoom in on Freddie with the speed of a decimating tornado. Handsome Harry's desire to devour was a love so intense that it demanded an immediate consummation.

Freddie didn't know what hit him. Handsome Harry came upon Freddie with the impact of a souped-up steel-plated Mack truck. There followed a crunch, and to Freddie's horror, one of his legs flew up into the air propelled by a geyser of blood; his mouth froze; wordless utterances gurgled out along with black bile. In the next split second came another crunch and he felt the grit of jagged teeth chewing upon his other leg. Then Freddie was tossed into the air like a child's rag doll, but one stuffed with blood, veins, arteries, bone and tissue mass, and whatever else in the way of edible meat could be found in a leg that had been severed above the knee.

"No! No! I don't want to die this way!" burbled Freddie as Handsome Harry's jaws locked onto Freddie's crotch, slitting his penis and scrotum in a surgical excision that, had Freddie escaped on his stumps, would have made a eunuch out of him, allowing him to be suitably in the employ of a brothel manageress to keep track of her inventory of fallen ladies. Freddie managed only to pop a few weak punches on the tip of Handsome Harry's snout as his sad corpse was dragged to the nearest waterway, along with twenty feet of his short intestine trailing down the path.

Handsome Harry finished hauling his cargo just as Cottonmouth made his appearance, slithered over to Freddie as he exsanguinated, and sunk his jaws into Freddie's neck, injecting him with paralyzing venom. A witness, had there been one been nearby, may have surmised that Cottonmouth had mercifully euthanized Freddie.

"Not you, too!" Freddie shrieked, while Cottonmouth reared his head and grimaced triumphantly in sync to the gurgling death rattle Freddie made in drawing his last breath. As though on cue from a higher authority, Cottonmouth curled the tip of his tail, signalling Handsome Harry to continue on his way, and give what remained of Freddie a proper blood-hued drenching in the stagnant brackish water, before gobbling up his long-awaited dream cuisine. But what he had to remember now was Cottonmouth's gustatory dictate: *Chew each piece slowly!*

Their Blissful Union

With Freddie completely out of the picture, Cottonmouth could do what he pleased with Hilda. He would see to it that she would never learn how her darling met his violent end. But Hilda's nostalgia often got the better of her. A few times, accompanied by Cottonmouth, she decided to come calling on Freddie, and not finding him at home, concluded that he had abandoned his ramshackle dwelling, and moved out of the area.

"Where could he have gone?" she asked, suddenly noticing what she assumed were blood stains on the kitchen floor. "Could he have met up with foul play?" she asked Cottonmouth, who, being the consummate actor, put on the saddest face his psyche could find in a pinch, and it looked genuinely mournful to Hilda. Gazing deeply into Cottonmouth's moistened eyes convinced her that he, too, was as saddened as she was by Freddie's departure out of their lives.

"You're missing him, honey?" twittered Hilda sweetly, brushing a tear away from her cheeks, to which Cottonmouth nodded his head in agreement.

Yet the stress of acting falsely before his honey started to make Cottonmouth nauseous. In truth, had Freddie become reincarnated as a round-tailed mouse, Cottonmouth would have flung it in the air, much like a cat would do playing with a squeak toy before devouring the creature head first, but unlike a cat going for quick nosh, Cottonmouth would instead go for the slowest digestive meal his gastro-system would allow him to relish.

"Where could he have gone?" she asked the master of cool. Cottonmouth shook his head, implying he hadn't a clue as to the matter of Freddie's disappearance, and for added emphasis, he managed to gush a few recycled tears, but not before a rush of acidulous nausea crept up the soft lining of his throat.

That acid reflux was sizzling like the surface of the Lake of Fire, or perhaps a few degrees hotter for lying reptiles. Had Hilda kept staring into Cottonmouth's peepers, she would have discerned a gleam of deceit. But being toxically in love with that double-dealing snake, she naturally erred in her judgement of him.

Dr. Copperhead would have prescribed a powerful laxative for her to excrete her infectious love stools. After all, she was part serpent, and enjoyed her shape-shifting snaky ways, even if true love was short-sighted.

"Wouldn't Freddie have wanted us to live here?" Hilda suddenly wondered aloud.

Again Cottonmouth nodded his agreement, hissing in delight that they would be setting up house together. That soiled pillow, however, would have to go. Cottonmouth was morbidly phobic on the issue of cleanliness. Nipping the offensive pillow between his gummy lips, he slithered out the door with it.

"Don't be away too long, honey," sighed Hilda. "I'm missing you already."

There was a darker reason, however, for Cottonmouth to dispose of that pillow. He feared that Gabriel would put in a call while he was away to reprimand him for taking part in Freddie's assassination, and what if the love of his life answered the pillow while he was on a hunt for the catch of the day to put on their dinner table? But it would then mean his villainy in Freddie's demise would be exposed to Hilda! It would be the end of their relationship and life's meaning for the rapacious snake.

"Bye, Honey, you hurry back soon!" Hilda called after him.

A frisson of fear rattled Cottonmouth's spine at the very thought of losing his precious Hilda. The situation called for an immediate whack job. That pillow had to be shredded in the same way he had once ripped apart Bruce, Freddie's prize snake tie. Cottonmouth knew exactly where to demolish the pillow; it was the usual place where Freddie used to bury those half-digested rodents which Cottonmouth hadn't finished eating. Freddie used to call the patch of ground where wild yellow swamp lilies flourished his "private little cemetery."

With the pillow torn apart beyond recognition, Cottonmouth hurried back to Hilda, his heart beating, his adrenaline on the high side, and as expected, she was reclining in bed, waiting for him, the viperish heat in her pulsating for the intense compressions that only Cottonmouth could provide. He greeted her with a mocking smile, suggesting that she would now be his to pleasure as she panted away for more and still more "squeezies."

Never were a nuptial pair so joyous. Later on, to further celebrate their blissful union, they planned to joyride on Handsome Harry's back throughout the waterways, that beast being forever grateful to Cottonmouth in setting up Freddie for him to devour. The musk of perfumed love was present in the fetid air.

Hisses, whispers, sighs and kisses, all coalesced to create the happiest of endings.

The Aftermath: An Apocalyptic Ending

It was a week like no other in Gorgonia when mortuary artist Laura née Dewberry was murdered by a cadaver, a former champion wrestler to whose wan face she was restoring some healthy flesh tones. On a whim, she sought to get pleasured by pouring some Fire Bull Surprise down the champ's throat, hoping to reanimate him a final time as a dynamo of a living stud. But instead of the carnal pleasure she sought, she was strangled.

But if this wasn't enough to send all of Gorgonia abuzz, rumours swirled about that its beloved mayor, Rufus Tbone LaMarr, a role model to the physically challenged, and himself a morbidly obese dwarf, was brazenly associating with high-profile criminals. His abnormally long hands drooping past his knees scooped up many a C-note, a few which he slipped into the hands of Annabelle Muerte, his dyspeptic receptionist – a reward for acting on his behalf as a loyal underling.

She suffered no fools, nor her boss's fools, and adding to her notoriety, some of her bedazzled co-workers claimed that she had actually memorized a rare first edition of *The Art of Insults*, authored by an obscure Victorian Canadian by the unlikely name of Thomas Albright Wainscot Schnauzer. Many a time when things weren't going well for Rufus Tbone LaMarr, a slow day, or no day for corruption, he put in a polite request to Annabelle to recite by rote a few of the choicest put-downs she relished, for his private amusement, and she did just that, and somehow it wafted away his saturnine vapours and made his day sunnier.

"Sugar doll," drawled Rufus Tbone LaMarr, "you sure are a real card."

"Why, thank you, Mr. LaMarr," giggled Annabelle, "you're so kind."

"Sweets," chortled Rufus Tbone LaMarr, "just call me Rufus, or...Roof."

"Okay, Mr. LaMarr, oops, oh dear me, oh dear me...I mean... Rufus."

"Now, that wasn't so hard, was it, my dear Annabelle? May I call you Bell?

"I wish you would, Mr. Rufus. Oh dear me, I mean Rufus, Bell, yes, yes."

"Well, Bell Titters, so I shall. I like the sound of Bell, rings off my tongue. Want to see some magic, Bell honey? One favour deserves another."

"Rufus, I'm so excited. Why, I feel like such a schoolgirl, I do."

"Watch this, Bell. Now, you keep a close eye on what I am going to do."

Fancying himself an awe-inspiring conjurer, a thorough professional in sleight-of-hand magic, Rufus Tbone LaMarr proceeded to tweak the lower lobe of his right ear and out from nowhere, it seemed, slid a newly minted silver dollar which he handed to Annabelle to keep, as a token indicating that he held her in the highest esteem, she being his special Bell.

"Oh, that is so neat," gushed Annabelle in bedazzlement.

But Annabelle was playing it sly as a cat fixated by a nest of newborn mice. She had one bit of wizardry which rattled Rufus Tbone LaMarr to the extent that he requested that she perform it, not in his midst but on some loathsome person who displeased her. From the safety of his office he had witnessed his Bell vigorously shaking the top of her head, and instantly the very ringlets of her reddish-brown hair would come alive, wriggling with noodle-thin hissing snakelets; predictably, the startled party fainted on the spot in a dead heap, much to Rufus Tbone LaMarr's delight, after which he began to wonder whether a malignant hiring agency in Deep Space had directed her to be employed by him.

Annabelle was her boss's first line of defence, and if by chance an intrepid soul slipped by her desk without first making an appointment to see him, Rufus Tbone LaMarr thought he had the perfect device to frighten off any individual bold enough to show up in his office: his secret weapon – a yellow cedar staff embossed with the carving of an entwining snake that appeared to meander up to a crystal skull of a handle, the size of a small doorknob. It came complete with a pair of green amber eyes radiating a fierce yellow light, and if that incandescence alone didn't do the trick of freezing an intruder, Rufus Tbone LaMarr was more than prepared to beat that interloper senseless. Still he had to take care that no blood of the person he had just coshed trickled down his office floor to ruin the fabric of his invaluable Persian carpet of the fifteenth-century Safavid Empire.

That carpet had been given to his Worship as a payoff by a developer who wanted him to pass some pesky building bylaws in Gorgonia. People with taste and knowledge in intricately hand-woven Oriental carpets always complimented Rufus Tbone LaMarr on his taste, even while they faced down his pet rod which he menacingly stroked with a religious fervency.

One afternoon, Rufus Tbone LaMarr suddenly stirred from his usual mid-afternoon office catnap, awoken by the whirr of wings and sunlight flashing across his brow. He assumed that the tall visitor staring down at him had drifted into his office when Annabelle was on her lunch hour. Gabriel's very presence illumed the interior of his large oak-panelled office, and the archangel further annoyed Rufus Tbone LaMarr by first making him feel even more diminutively challenged in height, and then defiantly fanning his translucent wings, as though wanting to waft away a bad smell. As well, Gabriel's luminescence had singed Rufus Tbone LaMarr's eyebrows, causing them to curl as if the devil himself had applied his special curling iron.

"Holy moly! I'm going off my front wheels. Stranger, who are you?"

"I see that you are fully aware of the Lake of Fire," sniggered Gabriel.

Rufus Tbone LaMarr reckoned that one of his subordinates on staff had hired some bit-part actor through central casting to maliciously spook him, and yet who among his staff would do such a damnable thing? Surely none of his employees bore a grudge against him. Hadn't they all shared in the largess of his bountiful dealings? As an equal opportunity employer, it made him teary-eyed.

"State your business, pal, and be quick about it. I don't have all day."

"Be more respectful of others. I am here on my Master's business."

"So what's with the feathers? Are you some kind of cross-dresser?"

"Enough!" gusted Gabriel. "I'm not to be addressed in this vulgar manner!"

"Now don't you get bent out of shape, but, hey, you do look like a weirdo."

"Fundament of Satan. Close your mouth. Do not speak! Nod, if you understand."

"Say, fellow, do you hide your balls under your feathers?"

"Your blighted soul begs to be free of corruption!"

"And I thought I had a runaway fart wanting to fly out of my arse."

"What a nasty being you are. You have the morals of a dung beetle."

"Hey, No-Nuts, want to see a trick?"

Whereupon he flung his staff on the office floor, and in a wink it turned into a snarling viper, which, had Rufus Tbone LaMarr known Cottonmouth, he would have sworn on a stack of stolen Holy Mormon Bibles was his likeness.

Gabriel, staring contemptuously at Rufus Tbone LaMarr, then threw his sacred lapis lazuli wand on the floor, and *tout de suite*, it changed into a massive firebrick red reptile with purply markings on its forehead. In seconds it had swallowed up the entire train of Rufus Tbone LaMarr's trophy serpent, along with some innards of its owner's self-esteem.

Humiliated in the extreme, he begged Gabriel to return his staff, which he did. Fang-marked, it lay there on the office table in quiet repose as though nothing out of the ordinary had transpired, but Rufus Tbone LaMarr knew better, his ego momentarily having been reduced in size to that of a pharaoh ant. But in his ignominious defeat, to prove he was made of sterner stuff, he dredged his psyche to come up with a kinder face to display to Gabriel, who suspiciously sniffed the villainy in the sinner.

That Rufus Tbone LaMarr was on the take was starkly evident, with Annabelle making a brief appearance in the office carrying a brown paper lunch bag brimming with greenbacks, which she hurriedly plunked down on his desk, cackling like an evil hen upon exiting from his office. Soon, Rufus Tbone LaMarr inhaled the fresh aroma of crisp C-notes in that bag with the same zest that a domestic pig might sniff the soil for truffles in some European forest.

"I suppose that lucre is from a criminal enterprise. Am I mistaken?"

"No, it's back city taxes owed in arrears by the Cygnus Sanitation Services."

"Venality runs through you like effluence in Hell. The Ocular sees all!"

"Ocular? Now about this Ocular you speak of, is it a magnifying glass?"

"The Ocular is the All-Seeing Eye which in obeisance serves my Master."

"You don't say," uttered Rufus Tbone LaMarr. "A see-all peeper. Wow!"

"My Master has seen the vile wickedness of the Gorgonians you serve."

"So, my exalted friend, you have a message for me from your Master?"

"I have, sir, a warning addressed to you and the citizens of Gorgonia."

"Look closer. Can't you see I'm all ears for your Master's message."

"First, I must insist that you remove that smirk from your deceiving lips."

"Give it to me straight. I can take it. I am ready, go ahead, shoot!"

"Very well then, pull in your ears, listen to what I have to say."

Once again Gabriel rustled his wings. The light of goodness and redemption settled over Rufus Tbone LaMarr`s face, blistering the tip his nose.

"You are to cease all communication and contact with the Azazel crime family. They are to close their illicit loan shark operations in Gorgonia and desist from dumping toxic waste and poisoning the ground water. The Oculus not only sees but hears the miniscule agonies of minnows and the loud croaking of suffering amphibians, and the death rattles of serpents, both large and small. Now as a condition of sparing Gorgonia from a plague that my Master will surely bring down on its fornicators, cretinous wastrels and worshippers of Mammon and their kind, my Master requests that you post a newsletter from your office to command those insufferable bounders in Gorgonia to surrender their banker boxes filled with negotiable bond and gold certificates, stacks of foreign currency, stolen credit cards, uncut diamonds, precious and semi-precious stones, all of which are to be delivered to Dr. Melon's mortuary, and unceremoniously cremated, And now to the matter of your fate and Annabelle's. I suggest that you both don protective aluminum pant wear, and padded aluminum jackets, wear aluminized hoods to fully cover your faces, aluminum goggles to protect your eyes, and for footwear, I suggest

aluminum-painted boots: please understand that no other metal-lic apparel will do. Fortunately, for both your sakes, the Oculus is unable to see through aluminum. And now onto another matter which rankles me. You are allowed to keep your ill-gotten acqui-sitions, my Master wishes it so, and yes, lest I forget, you may keep your carpet, which I gather isn't a divinely magic carpet woven for the purpose of lofting you high above the earth. Now onto another matter: My Master has instructed me that I am not to disclose the terrible plague which shall be inflicted on Gorgonia, should your Gorgonians go about their evil ways. One final matter, please inform your Annabelle that once you are out of Gorgonia, she is not to look back and witness its destruction. If she does turn, she will be transformed into a pillar of pig excre-ment, ripened with beetles, maggots and pestilential worms. Nod, if you understand. Do not speak! Do not speak."

But Rufus Tbone LaMarr was too transfixed to utter as much as a syllable. As Gabriel prepared to depart from the mayor's office, his humbled adversary, having regained his power of speech, beseeched Gabriel to urge his Master to spare Gorgonia, and allow a little time for the light of redemption to fall upon its inhabitants. Rufus Tbone LaMarr thought he would toss a zoological precept at Gabriel: if a snake, he reasoned, sloughed off its old skin and grew a new one, couldn't a Gor-gonian slough off an old venal skin and grow an incorruptible hide?

"Your request is denied! You and your scabbed kind are irre-deemable!"

"Is there no kindness in you? Have you no heart? Can't you see my tears?

"I have my orders. I serve my Master and no other standing by his Throne."

"I, too, follow orders. I serve the public, and no one stands by my throne."

"You say that you have a throne? And where may I ask is your throne?

"It's in the bathroom, you know, the John, and it's the flushing kind."

"Oh yes, your John. We don't waste water nor befoul it with excretions."

"You mean angels don't shit? You have no bowels or a set of balls?"

Not wanting to dignify that query which Gabriel found offensive, he invoked, instead, a magenta-coloured mist, and slipping into that heavenly cumulus, he disappeared from Rufus Tbone LaMarr's sight, leaving him to speculate whether Gabriel would issue a grievance against him and bring it to his Master's attention, or more pointedly, if that boss angel ratted him out to his Master would he end up fried to perfection in the Lake of Fire?

The mayor's newsletter, as requested by Gabriel, went out to all of Gorgonia. And it wasn't too long before Rufus Tbone LaMarr received a torrent of hate mail, his office phone rang off the hook, and Annabelle was swamped with calls for appointments, with some of the more vociferous individuals frightened away when she strenuously shook her head, directing a set of viperish curls in their direction. Several were savagely nipped by a few hissing curlicues, went into toxic shock, ended up writhing on the floor and expiring before Annabelle's desk.

What Rufus Tbone LaMarr feared most happened. It was a call from the Frank the Ice Man, accusing "Roofie" of skimming profits the mob made from their assorted illegal operations in loansharking and contract killings, super grass and sweet-scented crack cocaine. Roofie was a snow head, sniffing long lines of coke and this, combined with having Annabelle blow some angel dust into his face, was causing Roofie to go off his handrail, hallucinating, seeing angels, all the more strange because he had no known religious affiliations, and, worst of all, he was urging Gorgonians

to gather up their loot and transport it to a mortuary for crema-
tion. Squirrels were nesting in Roofie's head and they all had
babies and rabies. The job called for a nose, throat and ear spe-
cialist like Frank the Ice Man to clean out Roofie's ears with an
ice pick and waste those pesky squigglers.

Rufus Tbone LaMarr knew Frank's passion for removing ear
wax with a splash of brain attached. There was the temperament
of a sculptor in the man, bred in him by his grandfather, who
owned a fish-packing plant in New Jersey and let his grandson
chip away at fifty-pound blocks of ice, until all that was left of that
immense block were finely chopped splinters of ice.

Often, young Frank told the old workmates at the plant that
he wanted to become an ice sculptor at winter fairs, chopping
away at colossal blocks to create fanciful animals. His dream of
going to art school was never realized. Little did he know then
that his father and grandfather were working the early morning
hours for some moonshiners making gin, and had to keep the
primitive distillery tubes and vats in working order and the fire
and steam going under the copper kettles to conduct that white
lightning. They had a job for "Frankie": to take care of some rev-
enuers, put his talent with an ice pick to good use. Hence was
born the chilling sobriquet Frank the Ice Man, and Rufus Tbone
LaMarr was well-acquainted with Frank's background, which
was why he and Annabelle had to get out of Gorgonia armoured
in their aluminum apparel.

But should he take the time to inform his brother John that
he was leaving Gorgonia for good? He would leave John his
office carpet, knowing how much he fancied it and how he had
often said it would make a fine wall hanging for his recreation
room where he kept his billiard table.

The brothers weren't on the best speaking terms, with John
constantly urging him to go to rehab and take the cure for his var-
ied addictions, like snorting endless trails of coke via carefully

crafted tubes of greenbacks. And then there was his amazing bibulous power in polishing off a mickey of gin in the mid-afternoon. Yet, despite John's heartfelt pleas for his brother to reform, sadly, it all came to naught.

Rufus Tbone LaMarr had more immediate concerns relating to his health. He imagined being fast-frozen in the cargo hole of a fishing vessel, watching in terror as Frank performed a faux Newfoundland fisherman's jig, while chipping away at the ice-encased man whom he called Roofie, and taking pleasure in hearing the disjointed staccato rhythm of his ice pick, although never for a moment would he have ever considered himself a sculptor, yet the suffering aesthete in him yearned to be liberated.

There was a deep rumble of thunder from somewhere in the sky, a sound that one living on the prairies might associate with forked lightning. Rufus Tbone LaMarr, for some absurd reason, began musing that the rumbling in the clear blue mid-afternoon sky indicated a build-up of intestinal gas in some alimentary canal out in deep space.

Suddenly, a blast of seismic wind shook the ground he and Annabelle were standing on, and the sky above him turned as black as his widowed mother's frilly satin lace panties which she wore to bed, cradling him in her chubby arms, a practice which only ended when his mother, Bessie, found a younger lover in a befuddled lad of fifteen, the local paperboy, who proved malleably trainable to suit her urgent needs.

When the sky darkened, Rufus Tbone LaMarr and Annabelle were well out of range of Gorgonia, but something eerie was grabbing their attention and they were soon drawn to a captivating phenomenon – a silvery-hued orifice opening within the very fabric of the sky's dark matter. Some irrepressible force appeared to be at work, for what followed was something akin to a nuclear sneeze, followed in turn by a tornado force whoosh of flames, spewing forth wriggly creations not unlike Annabelle's wicked curlicues.

Fleeing the plague that was being visited upon Gorgonia, Rufus Tbone LaMarr remembered Gabriel's dictate: his Annabelle wasn't to witness Gorgonia's destruction, lest she turn into a pillar of excrement, and terrified of that horrid transmogrification of his cherished companion, he cautioned her to keep moving ahead.

"Don't you look back, sweet buns," he cried out, but it was all in vain, for what happened next would have even thrown Wonder Woman, his comic book super heroine, for a golden loop. Hearing the strains of *Scheherazade*, Nikolai Rimsky-Korsakov's, Opus 35 of his symphonic poem, Annabelle, a true audiophile, couldn't resist turning around to see what orchestra was playing that symphonic masterpiece, and wanting to get better view of those phantasmal musicians, she tore off her protective aluminum headpiece.

"It's a trick, no! No!" squealed Rufus Tbone LaMarr. A panic attack took hold of him. He found himself racing ahead in terror, a pathetic dwarfish figure of man, his lengthy arms swinging past his knees, swaying back and forth, while a pungent smell of excreted bodily waste followed him in his stride, ghosting up the vents of his nostrils into his sinus cavities. Having worked in an abattoir in his twenties before opting for the infinitely sweeter smell of public office, he was thoroughly acquainted with that stench.

Rufus Tbone LaMarr kept on running. Later on there would be sightings by climbers and their porters in the Himalayas of what appeared, at a distance, to be a dwarfish silvery ape with disproportionally long hands; the alpinists swore that the shiny critter they saw was related to the legendary hairy Yeti, a Himalayan version of the North American "Bigfoot." Alas, that diminutive figure of a resplendent Yeti may have met up with a sad end. A climber claimed to have witnessed him falling "ass over elbows" into a deep crevasse known as "the Big Swallow," but what really puzzled that witness was the offensive smell which greeted his nostrils shortly after that undersized monster fell to his death; by refusing to follow its master into the crevasse, it suggested to the living that it was not only invincible but had a consciousness all of its own, and as well, territorial ambitions to gain further air-space.

The sky's black pigment was being eaten away by flames, and in its place a rosy inferno predominated. It was a sight which would have electrified the muse of the Canadian bard, James Hogg. He would have viewed the magna flow of vipers falling from that aperture in that Stygian sky onto Gorgonia, as "the Himmler Solution," linking up the extinction of the Gorgonians with Gabriel's Master snuffing out the lives of the inhabitants of the Biblical cities, Sodom and Gomorrah, for the transgressions of a few low-life types who had made sexual advances to a band of touring angels.

Soon all of Gorgonia was swarming with combustible vipers, whose noxious gases alone sucked up all the available oxygen on the ground. Gorgonia was now free of humankind, an inspiring development for those earth bound reptiles looking to colonize the new Gorgonia once the magma on the ground cooled. They would then summon Cottonmouth and Hilda to their domain for a hush hush coronation ceremony, and the pair would thus become royalty.

Handsome Harry's eyes sparkled as he provided transport for their majesties through the murky waterways crowded with hordes of ecstatic reptiles that came out of hiding to celebrate the arrival of the royal couple. On the surface it appeared peaceful enough, yet something dark and ominous was smouldering beneath like a subterranean brush fire.

Now, Cottonmouth may have doffed a psychic crown of king-ship, but he, more than Hilda, knew what was raging in the hearts and minds of his subjects.

If Cottonmouth had his way, there wouldn't be any more pretty turtle shells on the shelves of curio shops, no snake or gator adorned leather shoes and boots sold in exclusive shoe emporiums, no penned-in gators readied to be slaughtered for their hide. All would be set free; as would gators trapped in suburban swimming pools of the super-rich, who, along with the gator hunters and fly-by-night waste management company employees illicitly dumping toxic waste near some pristine marshland nature preserve, would end up as some gobsmacked luncheon meat hurriedly devoured by gator foodies. Theirs was a meal that *schmecks*, all the more so, because the blood spurting from those chewed-up ne'er-do-wells provided clear exsanguinated gravy.

Cottonmouth wrapped himself tightly around Hilda, who murmured ecstatically for more compressions, while Handsome Harry, ever the faithful mode of transport, paddled away at such a breakneck pace that he would have put an Olympic swimmer to shame. Then something magical happened. A swell of air jetted between Handsome Harry's belly and the surface of the water, giving him the uplift of a catamaran. The two royals were thrilled to find they were flying above the water and being worshipfully acknowledged by a mass of reptilian onlookers, waving at them from below.

Another rush of air beneath Handsome Harry's belly, and it began to alarmingly dawn on him that some mysterious force was lifting him and his illustrious passengers well above the clouds. Suddenly, the blue of the sky was ripped apart by a gale force wind, which opened an immense hole in the firmament, and a golden light poured through, and then a monumentally enormous crocodilian head appeared in a blaze of liquid gold. Handsome Harry knew at once who that magnum monster confronting him was, and Cottonmouth knew as well, while Queen Hilda simply closed her eyes, wishing that it was a dream and that she and Cottonmouth were back on Freddie's soiled bed making whoopee.

That cosmic croc stared down glaring delightfully at the three. A storm of tears, tears of joy, soon gushed from the corners of his violet blue eyes.

Kungakamuzuzi, the Crocodilian God of the Heavens, hissed out a thunderous post-nuptial blessing for the royal couple, and the force of this exhalation sent the three whirling back towards earth. In their descent, they discerned what appeared to be a hyper-sweet smile on the tip of the snout of that supernal beast just before he disappeared, and that aperture, which had been his window, was quickly filled in with an effervescent blue dye.

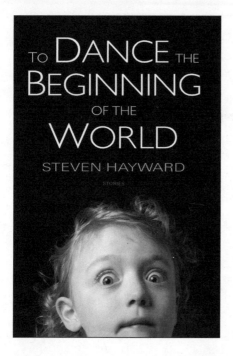

March 2015

Erudite and funny, nostalgic and fanciful, these stories unlock the secret longings and unlooked for victories that make up everyday life. Whether he finds himself in the stands at Yankee Stadium on Bat Day, or, as in "Aunt Daisy's Secret Sauce for Hamburgers" caught off guard by the myriad ways in which a recipe and its misspellings are a window into the woman who wrote it years before, or gently exploring how loss and love get intertwined for a "Bee Girl," Hayward writes with a sure sense of his characters and the complex, imperfect worlds they inhabit. Talent and passionate complexity have created an elegant and unforgettable collection of stories that are assured in depictions of characters and distinctive in voice.

Steven Hayward's first book, a collection of short fiction entitled *Buddha Stevens and Other Stories,* won the Upper Canada Writer's Craft Award in 2001 and was named by the *Globe and Mail* as one of the top 10 Canadian books of that year. His novel, *The Secret Mitzvah of Lucio Burke,* won Italy's Premio Grinzane Cavour Prize for best first novel, and his next, *Don't Be Afraid,* was a *Globe and Mail* Best Book for 2012 and a Canadian national bestseller. Born in Toronto, he currently teaches in the English Department at Colorado College, in Colorado Springs.

March 2015

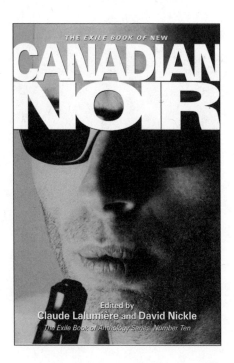

THE *EXILE* BOOK OF NEW

CANADIAN NOIR

Edited by
Claude Lalumière and **David Nickle**
The Exile Book of Anthology Series, Number Ten

Noir has never been a genre so much as a tone, an overlay, a mood, and this anthology resists the temptation to define what is meant by *noir* – the editors were much more interested in what it meant to Canadian writers. In *New Canadian Noir* the full spectrum of the noir esthetic is explored: from its hard-boiled home in crime fiction to its grim forays into horror, fantasy, and surrealism; from the dystopian shadows it casts in science fiction to the mixture of desire and corruption it brings to erotica; from the blood-spattered romance of the frontier to the stark nihilism of literary realism.

Major cities like Montreal, Toronto, Vancouver, Halifax, and Calgary provide location – while regions such as Nunavut and the Okanagan Valley offer natural settings – for stories like those of an elderly widow who ekes out a living collecting detritus while seeking to avenge the murder of her friend, a love-weary security guard who clashes with bounty hunters, an ursine meth-cooker who faces even stranger creatures on the frozen tundra of Nunavut, and the dead walking while the living despair as a private detective unravels a bizarre mystery.

This remarkable collection of poems lures you in, at first to stand alone in the dark… but slowly there comes a hint of light from a crack beneath a door. Then a riot of sensuous intensity as you open up to the beauty that lies between the folds of words, bursts of poetic energy that casts warm light over all shadows.

Jeff Bien's earlier poetic work has been called "a display of verbal pyrotechnics such as I've never seen before" by the late Irving Layton; "Potent and persuasive" by Lawrence Ferlinghetti, from *City Lights*, San Francisco; "of great merit" by Nobel nominee Charles Bliss, in addition to having been recognized by Ted Hughes, and Seamus Heaney, in selecting his work for the *Arvon Anthology* of Great Britain. A review written for *Poetry Canada* cited "a major voice has emerged, there is greatness in his work."

Jeff Bien of Kemptville, Ontario, is an internationally acclaimed poet, musician, meditation and spiritual practitioner. His work has been published, translated and performed in more than thirty countries. He is the author of numerous books which have received critical acclaim in Canada and abroad, and his poetry has been the recipient of many awards. Along with this newest collection of poetry, he is completing two new books of prose, *Songs of Non-Separation: Teachings on Consciousness and Spirituality*, and *Undressing the Illusion: Letters to a Young Mystic*.

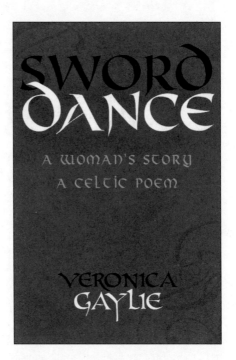

SWORD
DANCE

A WOMAN'S STORY
A CELTIC POEM

VERONICA
GAYLIE

A woman's childhood life in Scotland and a new life in Canada are explored by her daughter in this memoir-style poem that profoundly embodies the classic Canadian immigrant tale.

The story opens with Tom, Dick and Harry, three ancestors who emigrated to New York. It cycles back to the author's father, a young soldier who catches the eye of his wife-to-be at the glove counter in Woolworth's. In between we encounter the real, rare characters of everyday Glasgow life, including cousin John Lennon in a scheme to raise pigs, and a bicycle riding Richard Nixon who arrives just after a factory blow-up.

Framed by a prologue and epilogue, the story is told in a working-class vernacular – the characters all real, the voice gritty, witty and distinct as it unfurls a beautiful tapestry by way of the music and language of Glaswegian storytelling.

Veronica Gaylie is a poet, writer, teacher and environmentalist from Vancouver. Her work has been published in literary journals around the globe, including *Poetry Review* (UK), *Crannog* (Ireland), and the Canadian journals *Geist, Grain, Geez, Lake, Ditch, Room, Carte Blanche, Filling Station* and *ELQ/Exile: The Literary Quarterly*. Recently, she has been reading her essays for CBC Radio Sunday Edition. Veronica's heart belongs to Glasgow, though her soul wanders on Canadian mountains and Irish peninsulas. *Níl gach uile fhánaí caillte.*

Annual Literary Competitions
(open to Canadians only)

Exile's $15,000 Carter V. Cooper Short Fiction Competition

$10,000 for the Best Story by an Emerging Writer
$5,000 for the Best Story by a Writer at Any Career Point

The 12 short-listed are published in the annual *CVC Short Fiction Anthology*
and the Canadian journal *ELQ/Exile: The Literary Quarterly*

Exile's $2,500 Gwendolyn MacEwen Poetry Competition

$2,000 for the Best Suite of Poetry
$500 for the Best Poem

Winners are published in *ELQ/Exile: The Literary Quarterly*

Details and Entry Forms at
www.TheExileWriters.com